Trapped in Time

Denise Daye

DEDICATION

For Mom

(Just skip over the love scenes, please)

Don't forget to sign up for our newsletter to get FREE romance novels. You can find the newsletter and more info about our books here:

www.timelesspapers.com

Thank you!

TABLE OF CONTENTS

CHAPTER 1

Why did I agree to this in the first place? Emma looked up at the young man who was barely old enough to make the drink in his hand legal. *This party is a bad idea. I knew it the moment Lisa invited me.* Her friend had pressured her for weeks, and she had finally given in after Lisa helped her on a paper for their biochemistry class.

"So? Would you like to dance?"

Emma did another peek around the room. Her gaze paused for a few seconds on a group loudly cheering on a girl who was chugging down a big glass of beer. She looked about fifteen, half Emma's age.

"I'm so sorry, but my boyfriend is just using the bathroom. He'll be right back."

"That boyfriend must have a bad case of diarrhea. He's been gone since you arrived two hours ago."

Ouch. People here are young and drunk but not stupid. The young fellow took off again, back into the crowd, which was now dancing wildly to overly loud hip-hop. Emma straightened her dress at her waistline. Praise be for choosing her dark-blue, ankle-long dinner dress over the sexy red cocktail dress. That guy had been the sixth one to come over and bother her. Yes, "bother" was the right word, as the other five had been so drunk that one of them had fallen on her. And none of them had accepted a polite "No, thank you."

Emma was a beauty in her own way. Her strawberry-blonde hair and green eyes were not the usual colors folks saw around here, and she had a slim figure that was curvy where it needed to be. With clear and strong features, her face had a noble beauty to it that was noticed instantly by the other sex—and her own sometimes too.

Wait. Did he say two hours? Had she been sitting here sipping wine and fighting off drunks for that long? Well, at least that would explain why she felt so tipsy. She'd been generous with herself from that never-ending wine supply from the moment she arrived. It was time to go home. Especially now that Lisa was nowhere to be seen. Per the norm, she'd disappeared with some handsome frat boy early on in the party. That usually resulted in unanswered texts, followed by an apology the next morning. Not that it bothered Emma. Quite the opposite. She admired Lisa's carefree attitude and was almost a bit jealous of her ability to live life like there was no tomorrow — every darn day.

Emma hadn't been with a man in years. Not because she couldn't have one; they were lining up at her door. No…it was the fault of none other than her father. The one man who was supposed to love her and protect her unconditionally had not only let her down but was also the cause for her deep distrust of men. For years, she had watched him abuse her mother, and for years, she'd sworn to herself she would never marry and let a man treat her like that. Of course, she dated, but nothing serious. She always made it clear that she wasn't looking for anything more than a short-term encounter, and she did an excellent job at picking the kind of guys who understood that perfectly. But even her so-called short-term encounters had become tiresome. She was growing older and starting to realize that she needed a certain connection to a man in order to let him touch her. Unfortunately, she'd yet to find that sort of connection.

Emma wrapped herself tightly with her coat to protect herself from the cold breeze that awaited her outside. It was late, and not many people were still on the streets. But she didn't live far, so she decided to walk. The happy voices from the party started to fade as each step brought her closer to home. The good thing about living in her university's district was the proximity to everything. Sure, the rent was expensive, even with several roommates, but she didn't mind the roommate situation at all. It allowed her to live within walking distance of her school and her part-time job as a pharmacy technician.

She'd grown up poor. Very poor. Food stamps, secondhand clothing, the constant struggle of turning every penny twice. She'd been a smart kid, so nobody was surprised when she finished her training as a pharmacy technician. Not that she had grown up wanting nothing more than to work at a pharmacy. Who does? But she did have a love for chemistry and science and enjoyed working in that field. It inspired her. And this tech position was an easy way out of her mother's poverty-ridden studio.

After her mother finally left her abusive father, they lived below the poverty level, so she and her mother had had to share a studio together. Emma had slept on the couch, and her mother had slept on a mattress on the floor next to her.

In Emma's quest to get out of there, she'd applied for a job at her local pharmacy and had been thrilled when she got it. It wasn't a lot of money, but it was enough to get her own studio and pay her own bills. Sometimes, she even had enough left over to help out her mother.

Years passed by, and Emma lived contentedly as a pharmacy tech. Or, at least she'd thought she was content. The day after Thanksgiving, four years ago, Emma made the decision to go back to school to be more than a tech. She remembered the moment the desire struck like it was yesterday. She'd been taking over the register when the mean-kid incident happened.

"Mean Kid," as she called him, was one of those children nobody liked. He was at the store with his father, who seemed totally overwhelmed by his unruly child. Emma watched the boy run through the store, screaming like a wild animal. He must have been eight or so but acted like he was two. He had chocolate around his mouth and was still in pajamas. Emma had just filled the mean boy's prescription—antibiotics for an ear infection—and handed them to his dad when the tornado in Lightning McQueen pajamas came running to the pharmacy counter and decided to be, well, mean.

"Daddy, what is this woman doing?"

"She works here."

"What does she do?"

Emma leaned over the countertop. "I make people better with medicine." She thought that sounded pretty kid-friendly, and even a bit like she was important. But Mean Kid totally ignored her like she didn't exist.

"Daddy, is she a doctor?"

"I don't know, sweetheart."

"No, I am a pharmacy technician."

"Then how can you make me better?" Mean Kid screamed at Emma. Some customers stopped to look at the action going on.

"Well, I can give you this medicine, and it will make you better," she said, forcing herself to smile.

"Do you make my medicine?" Mean Kid yelled.

"No, but—"

"Your work is stupid! You're stupid!" he shouted at her and ran off again.

Emma had accepted the father's apology, and that should have been that. But, for some reason, it wasn't. She'd lain awake that night, thinking about her job and whether it was what she truly wanted to be for the rest of her life.

The answer was no.

She was grateful for her job, but what about her dreams of going to college? Mean Kid had done it. The mean kid had sent her back to school. She wouldn't become a physician—odds to make it into med school were not in her favor—but she could be the person who made the medicine. She could be a pharmacy scientist. She had always loved chemistry and was a hard worker. So, why not? Why not step it up with a PhD in pharmacy?

So, here she was. Four years into her bachelor's in pharmaceutical science and on her way home from a college frat party. She was almost twice as old as most of the other students in her class—another reason she didn't like to hang out at those parties.

Emma finally saw the steps to her house. She was about to get her keys out of her purse when something shiny caught her attention. Without much thought, she changed course and walked toward the shiny object, right onto the small one-way street in front of her house. It reflected the streetlights like a little disco ball. *Must be a coin or something*. She was right on. It was some sort of coin someone must have dropped in the middle of the road.

"A good luck coin," she mumbled to herself.

She bent over to grab it and noticed instantly that it wasn't an American coin. It had some sort of queen on it and almost looked European. Kind of old. She held it up against the glow of the streetlights hanging above her, but the lights were too dim to read its etched letters. She was about to get her cell out to use as a flashlight when, out of nowhere, light flooded her from behind like a tsunami hitting the shores. She knew exactly what kind of light it was. Emma felt a cold flood of fear rushing through her body. She moved instinctively, but too late—no chance to shout, jump, or pray. She didn't even get to see the car.

Everything went black. She heard squeaking wheels and a car horn. For a few seconds, she felt pain like she had never felt before. Then there was nothing but darkness and her fearful thoughts. *Is this it? Is this how people die?* Then even the darkness disappeared, and she passed out.

CHAPTER 2

Emma felt a weird movement in the right hand pocket of her coat. She had a terrible ringing in her ears that slowly gave way to street noises, and her head hurt something awful.

"Hey! Leave her alone, you stinking drunk!" a woman's voice shouted in a Cockney accent.

Emma slowly opened her eyes. A dirty man was leaning over her, going through her pocket. His smell was so repulsive, she kicked out at him, more in response to the stench than the fact that he was robbing her.

"Get away from her!" the woman yelled again.

Emma looked over and spotted her savior, a woman in her late twenties. She came barreling towards them like a train ready to run over its victim. The man jumped up and tried to run away with Emma's purse in his hand, but the purse's straps were still around Emma's neck. The purse snapped right out of his hands and back into Emma's lap. Rather than running away, the man stood for a second and stared at Emma in confusion, like he'd never seen a purse with straps before.

"What the bloody hell?" he spat in her direction before disappearing behind a horse-drawn carriage rattling by.

Wait — what! A horse-drawn carriage? Emma stared at the carriage in disbelief until it vanished around a street corner.

"Are you all right, dear? You are bleeding from your head." The woman who'd come to her rescue now leaned over her and grabbed Emma under her arm, helping her to her feet.

Emma touched her head wound and then looked at her hand. There was blood, but it looked dry. She turned unsteadily to the woman.

What the hell was she wearing? Her rescuer was dressed like a lady out of a period drama. Her clothes seemed to be made out of some sort of green and brown wool. It wasn't one of the huge dresses worn in the Marie Antoinette movies, but it was still a period garment. The woman's brown hair was put up into a lazy bun. She was a bit on the heavier side but not bad looking. Her makeup was way over the top though.

Emma promptly panicked. "We need to call nine-one-one. A car hit me. I think I have a serious brain injury or something," she said, moving her hands up and down to stop herself from hyperventilating.

Now it was the lady's turn to look at Emma with all the curiosity in the world.

"What is a car? And who is this 'nine-one-one' you speak of?"

A couple walked by and scanned Emma with a strange expression on their faces. The man wore a top hat and a noble period suit. The woman was dressed similarly, their attire far finer than the woman who'd just chased away the thief guy. Another carriage passed by.

Emma had had enough of this! She obviously needed medical attention for a concussion—or worse—and these people weren't helping at all.

"Fine. I'll call nine-one-one myself!" She reached into her purse and thanked God that, for once in her life, she'd left the house with her cell fully charged. She swiped across the screen, her fingers shaking, and dialed 911, but the call didn't ring through. Busy signal. She hung up and dialed again. Same problem. The cause revealed itself in the form of no bars.

"I'll just have to restart it," Emma spoke aloud. Her hands were so unsteady, she had to push the button several times in a row. What was going on here?

"I have never seen a music box like this before. And your dress…you are not from here, are you?" the woman asked, her brows raised high.

Emma rolled her eyes.

"Well, obviously, I'm American, as we're in—" She stopped talking and quickly analyzed the street again. Now that she looked closer, it didn't look like Philadelphia at all. Not even a Philadelphia in some period drama.

"Is this still America? Twenty-first-century America?" Emma asked in total shock.

"No, this is London…1881, to be exact."

Did she say London in 1881? Emma tried to call 911 again, but she still had no signal. She walked a few steps to the left and held her phone up as high as she could but, again, no signal. This was too much. Emma had never been someone who cried over everything and nothing, but this was more than even she could handle. She threw her head into her hands in desperation.

The woman put a comforting hand on Emma's shoulder. Emma wanted to remove her hand, but the gesture of kindness was appreciated, and the woman seemed sincere. As if she truly felt for her.

"Well, well, now, please don't cry. It is getting dark. How about we go to my room for now and see what we can do about all of this tomorrow morning? It looks like something terrible happened to you, and you need to rest. Maybe a coach ran into you? These bloody postal coaches almost got me twice last week."

Emma looked at the woman. She was lost here, wherever here was, and needed medical attention but had no idea how she could make it to a hospital in the state she was in.

"My name is Lily," the friendly woman said. "I live not far from here. This is not a place for a woman after dark, and it is getting awfully late. See?" Lily pointed to a man who was using some sort of a ladder to light the street's lanterns. Emma hated to admit it, but this Lily was right; no place was a good place for her to be out alone with a brain injury.

"Emma," she said in a voice that sounded more like a discouraged whisper.

"All right, Emma. Let us go before that thief comes back with his vazey friends for that fancy handbag of yours. These rats are creatures of the night, and the police do not patrol this part of town at night. Too busy protecting the fancy folks down in Kensington."

"Yes, of course. Thank you." She thought it best to play along for now, until things started to make sense again. Which would hopefully be tomorrow morning, after a good night's rest. *The lantern man doesn't do a very good job*, Emma thought as the streets in front of them grew dark within a matter of minutes.

On the way to Lily's room, Emma saw the craziest things. People pushing carts, horse carriages, children begging in the streets, prostitutes pressing themselves against potential customers, who either pushed them away or disappeared with them in the dark, and everybody was seemingly dressed appropriately for the Victorian time period.

Lily's room was in a terrace house on a street that looked exactly like those sketchy neighborhoods in period movies where people would die of some sort of bronchitis in the streets. The smell was beyond terrible, and the ground was wet and muddy, soaking Emma's feet in a brown substance she hoped was anything but feces.

Lily unlocked the door to a room on the second floor of an old, musty building that was filled with tenants. *A good night's rest might not be happening, after all.* Lily's room turned out to be a tiny room the size of an American master bath. It was empty—and not empty as in no cozy pictures or décor. Empty as in there was nothing in the room but a table that had a washbasin on it, a wood stove, and a small closet. Lily skipped by Emma proudly and opened her arms in the middle of her little paradise.

"This is it! My very own flat. I just got it last month and already have a visitor!"

Emma tried to be polite. Lily had been so kind to her. What kind of person would she be to insult her?

"It looks—great!"

"It's not grand, but it is much better than those flea-infested potato sacks that the pimps and brothel owners make you sleep on." Lily put a log into the wood-burning stove that by no means would pass any inspection in the twenty-first century and spread a blanket out on the floor big enough for the two of them to sleep on.

"If we sleep close to the stove, we shall be warm all night." She reached into the bag she had around her shoulders and pulled out chunks of bread and cheese. She handed them to Emma. "Here, you must be hungry, you poor thing."

Emma accepted and tried to take a bite of the bread, but it was so hard, she was worried about breaking a tooth. The cheese was easier to chew but most likely not pasteurized. Emma almost laughed out loud as she silently thanked her mother for the many times she'd taken Emma dumpster diving at night in grocery store parking lots to look for food that was past its expiration date. At first, some of the dumpster food had given her a tummy ache, but that had gone away pretty quickly, and her system overall seemed to have gotten used to digesting expired food. And now, here she was, standing in the middle of an empty room next to a woman who was most likely a Victorian prostitute, thanking her mother for making her eat expired food so she wouldn't get sick from eating unpasteurized cheese in 1881.

Lily knelt on the blanket to make a pillow out of a skirt. Emma watched her as she moved about. This woman had been so incredibly kind to

Emma; without her, she would have been lost and robbed. Emma sat down next to her.

"Thank you, Lily. You saved me tonight."

"Ah, of course. Tomorrow, we shall figure things out. You can stay here for as long as you need to call on that Mr. Nine-one-one again. Maybe the police can help you find this Mr. Nine-one-one?"

Emma smiled. Mr. Nine-one-one.

"Yes, I think tomorrow will be a lot easier. I might just need to rest. I think I hurt my head, and with a bit of sleep, things might get back to normal." Whatever normal was at this point.

"Hopefully. What do you do for a living? Are you married? You certainly do not look like you are one of us wagtails."

Emma didn't want to be rude, but no, she wasn't a Victorian prostitute, so she didn't say anything. Lily was a smart cookie and noticed Emma's hesitation to respond.

"Do not worry. I never thought you a fallen lady. You definitely do not look like a factory girl, either. To be honest, you do not quite look like anything I have ever seen before," Lily said, studying Emma from head to toe. "No, not a prostitute. It is obvious that you have not done any form of hard labor a day in your life." Lily grabbed Emma's hands and turned them around. "See. Soft as a baby's arse. They give you away." Lily smiled, offering Emma her hand to confirm what hard labor looked like.

Upon closer inspection, Lily's hands felt rough and looked like the hands of a woman in her fifties.

"You're right. I'm not a prostitute or a factory girl. I've worked hard in my life but not with my hands. I'm...I'm a..." Shoot. What should she say now? Lily probably had no idea what a pharmacist was, not to mention a university student. Sure, in Emma's world, there was nothing to it for a woman to go to school, but wherever she was now seemed to be long before the time of the women's rights movement.

Lily seemed to have quite the talent for knowing what Emma was thinking. "You can tell me. I shall not think you mad or laugh. That music box alone would make me believe anything you say."

Emma contemplated. What did she have to lose? Lily wouldn't throw her out or send her to an insane asylum in the middle of the night. She seemed too kind for that. Plus, she'd probably seen and heard a lot worse in her line of work. The worst she could do was laugh at Emma and ask her to leave in the morning.

"Well, I used to work at a shop where I would sell medicine."

"Like a druggist?"

"Yes, if that's what you call it here. But now I am going to school to become a person who makes medicine."

"Like a chemist?"

Emma nodded her head.

"And that is allowed for women where you come from?"

"Yes, it is. Where I'm from, it's not unusual for a woman to go to university or work at a shop."

"Here, people would laugh at women for trying to go to school to become a chemist. I was not always a prostitute, you know. I used to live on a farm back when I was still married. But my husband was an awful man. He drank and beat me something rotten. It was so bad, some nights I wanted to be gone. Thin air, the river, you name it, as long as it was away from him. One day, I just woke up and left. I do not remember how I found the courage, but I just did it. Just left. I was unable to find work that would pay enough for me to live on my own. A teacher's salary is not enough to pay for a flat. Many do not know it, but most of us can read and write." She shrugged her shoulders and turned back to stoke the fire in the stove. "We are forced to do this line of work to survive. Nothing else pays a woman enough to be free of a drunk wife beater."

Lily's words made Emma sad. This woman was nothing but kindness and selflessness, and yet here she was, prostituting herself out to live in an empty place, sleeping on the floor like a dog. But to Emma's surprise, Lily laughed out loud.

"Do not look at me like that. It is not that bad! I work for myself, no pimps. I am free, and at least now I get to choose when I want to spread my legs, which I had no choice over when I was still married."

Emma couldn't help but admire Lily. What a positive way to look at things. Especially after everything Lily had been through. She was a true fighter.

"But enough for today. Let us sleep. You need to rest. I am sure it hurt when this Mr. Car hit you. Maybe tomorrow, you can tell me more about that fellow. I know everything there is to know about pricks. Believe me."

Emma couldn't deny she was beyond tired, but a quiet chuckle escaped when Lily mentioned "Mr. Car." She almost felt regret that she wouldn't get to know her most likely imaginary friend better when she woke up in a hospital bed tomorrow morning. In America, USA, twenty-first century.

"Goodnight, Lily. And thanks again for everything." Emma stretched out on the floor and tried to find a comfortable position, something easier said than done. The floor was hard as a rock. Heck, maybe it was a rock; it was too dark for Emma to tell.

"Goodnight, Emma," Lily mumbled, half-asleep.

Life for a woman in 1881 must not have been easy—if you were poor. What would Emma do if her life, or head state, or whatever this was didn't return to normal tomorrow?

Nah, she thought, convincing herself it was all in her head. A coma, maybe. A concussion, for sure. Both preferable to any possibility she was actually sleeping on a cold, hard floor next to a kind prostitute in 1881 London. *Things will be just fine in the morning. Back to normal. Back to the twenty-first century.*

It was already bright out when Emma slowly woke to the sound of people talking in the streets. To her surprise, she'd slept pretty good, considering she passed out on a hard floor next to a wood stove in Victorian London—

"No way!" Emma shouted aloud in panic, tumbling to the window. She pressed her face against the glass so hard it hurt. There it was! Victorian London!

Behind her, Lily rolled over and rubbed her eyes. "Are you feeling better?"

Feeling better? Emma fell backward and landed hard on her butt. At this point, there was really no use denying it any longer. Traumatic brain injury, insanity, or time travel. Whatever was going on obviously *was* going on. This was

Victorian London in 1881. And Emma was trapped in it.

"Emma...are you feeling better?" Lily put a hand on her shoulder.

"Y...y...yes..." Emma bit her lip, sinking deeply into her thoughts again. How could she get back home? She had no clue. Somehow, she would need to find out what was going on and how she could get back home, but for now, she would have to find a way to survive first. This place was no joke. Emma looked over to Lily, who looked like she was still waiting for an answer from her.

"What was that, Lily?" It was supposed to sound normal, but to her ears, it had come out sounding totally fake.

"Do you have anywhere to go?" Lily asked.

Emma shook her head, feeling like a sad puppy.

"Money?"

Sad puppy face again.

"Family...?"

Nope.

"…friends?" Lily seemed to interpret Emma's silence to that question as another no. She walked over to Emma. "You have me now. I shall be your friend. You hear me?"

Stunned by Lily's kindness, Emma barely got out a grateful nod.

"So, we shall find you employment today. You could always consider my line of work. With your looks and American accent, you could make it into the finest brothels in no time. Customers love exotic women."

Exotic? Emma was from the United States of America, not the moon. But the point was moot. The thought of giving her body up to fat old men for a few coins repulsed her.

"I mean no offense, Lily, but I would rather try other things first."

"None taken. I already knew that this would not work for you. You could always sell that music box of yours. Could fetch you a fortune with the right buyer."

Emma had already thought of that herself, but would it be wise to do that? Who knew—it might be the very thing that would get her back home.

"No, I'm sorry. I really need to get back home."

"I thought so. What is it, anyway?"

Emma grabbed it out of her purse and handed it to Lily, who accepted it into her hands like she was holding a holy relic. She tapped the touchscreen and almost dropped it in awe when the screen turned on, lighting up the room with a picture of Emma and her dog Winnie, who passed away two years ago.

"It is magic!" an excited Lily shouted, hopping from one leg to the other.

"Not really. It's technology. Where I'm from, everybody has one." Emma thought it better to take it back before Lily dropped it.

"How amazing! None of the inventions the newspapers scream about daily even come close to this box. It could make you rich!"

Emma turned it off to preserve the battery and put it back into her purse.

"I know, but it will be of more use to me if I keep it. I know it. You can't tell anybody about it. Ever. If it were to be taken from me—I am not sure I would ever find my way home again."

"I shan't," Lily promised, still in awe over her magic music box.

Now that the sale of her phone was off the table, Emma needed to find a job that would make her enough money not only to survive but also to allow her the freedom to do research. Research on anything that could possibly help her understand what was going on here. Medical journals, scientists, psychiatrists, time travel, goddamn ancient aliens, if need be, but she needed to find a way back home ASAP.

"What kind of work allows you freedom but also provides you with enough money to do research, maybe even attend college?"

The corners of Lily's lips drew down. That wasn't a good sign. "I shall be as honest with you as I can, Emma. If there is a time in which women will be free to do the things you asked for, this is not it. When I left my husband, I tried many different things to survive. I do not have the education that you do, but I have other talents, and I can read and write. For a woman not part of society, there are only two ways to have enough money to be free and to be allowed to do even the slightest amount of academics privately…"

That triggered some hope in Emma. "What are they?"

"One, you rejected."

"Oh…" Emma's hope deflated a bit. "And the other one?"

"Well, you would only be slightly free. More free with some than others, if you know what I mean?"

Emma didn't have to think long to answer that question. Of course. How the hell did she not guess that right away? Every darn period romance novel her mother ever touched was about this exact thing. The one thing Emma swore to herself to stay away from. *Marriage, damn it!*

From a historical point of view, it made total sense. Women had no rights. None whatsoever. The only women who had the time and money to do studies of any sort were either rich by birth or married to money. So those were her options in Victorian London in 1881. Prostitution or marrying into money. As terrible as they both sounded, she already knew in her heart which one she would be able to pull off in no time like a champ, and judging from the grin on her face, Lily thought so as well.

CHAPTER 3

"Not the pink one," Antoinette shouted arrogantly, waving her hand fan dramatically as though she were on a theater stage. Like a beaten dog, Emma hung the pink dress back into Antoinette's collection of the latest Victorian fashion. Lily knew Antoinette from years back. They had arrived in London around the same time and had shared a room together for a few months. But unlike Lily, Antoinette's noble looks and perfect figure had instantly landed her a spot in one of the best brothels in town, which had clearly rubbed off on her.

After hours of debating, Antoinette had finally agreed to trade one of her dresses for the fake diamond necklace and earrings Emma had been wearing the night she was hit by the car. At least, she was pretty sure she'd been hit. She had decided not to question all the mysteries surrounding that night and to only focus on survival and getting home.

For twenty-first-century standards, the set was pretty but made in China for less than a dollar. In 1881, however, before machines replaced humans to reach new levels of perfection in production standards, the set was considered one of the highest levels of replica and could be mistaken for real. Lily and Emma had played with the idea of selling it under pretense, but then Emma didn't feel right tricking people like that. Luckily for both of them, Antoinette had taken an instant liking to the set, fake or not, dancing in it in front of her countless mirrors and singing loudly.

"The pink one is from Lord Warrington, and he is so very peculiar about my wardrobe when he visits."

"You mean Lord Warrington, also known as Sucking Willy?" Lily asked with a grin.

"Who is Sucking Willy?"

"Every prostitute in London knows Sucking Willy. He wears nappies during his visits and wants to suck your titty like a little baby." Emma and Lily laughed out loud, much to Antoinette's annoyance; she did not share their humor.

"Hurry up now, will you? I have customers waiting!"

"Well, if not the pink one, then how about the green one? It looks delightful on you, Emma," Lily said, trying not to laugh again.

The green dress was not as extravagant as the pink one, but it was still a hand-tailored dress from the finest shop in London. It was short in the front and on the sides, just barely covering Emma's feet, and had a heavily decorated tail in the back. Antoinette had been sure to boast it was peak fashion.

"Sure, take it and go. And do not tell a soul about this. I want people to think these diamonds are real!" Antoinette's last words ushered Emma and Lily rudely out onto the street, the trussed-up prostitute slamming the door behind them.

The visit had gone rather well in Emma's mind, aside from Antoinette's attempt to talk Emma into hiring her as Emma's pimp. Emma's slim-but-healthy feminine curves boosted her potential for popularity to the very top in looks by Victorian standards. Her strawberry-blonde hair and green eyes were uncommon around here as well. Back home, Emma had been considered exceptionally pretty, but here, in period London, she seemed to be a whole different level of beautiful.

"Is that all we need?" Emma asked, looking about the busy Victorian street she was standing in like it was all a dream.

"I have a few more things to take care of now, but we should be ready by the morning."

Emma wrinkled her forehead. This was all going so fast! It had barely been a week, and tomorrow seemed awfully close to pull off their master plan.

"Why don't we wait a bit longer to work on the plan in more detail—heck, maybe even re-think the whole thing?" Emma asked in a voice that clearly exposed her doubts.

Lily started walking, briskly dodging pedestrians and chaos with practiced ease. "Because I do not have enough money to feed us for another day, even if we skip breakfast and lunch again. I already missed work today, which means no food today and tomorrow. We need to get you out of here as soon as we can. We do not want people to see you walking around for too long and start asking questions about who you are. There are not that many American beauties around here."

That all made sense to Emma, and she felt bad once again for taking so much gratuity from Lily.

The guilt of taking food from her mouth had Emma hunching her shoulders as she followed in her friend's wake, but it didn't change the fact that she did not feel ready for any of this. But then, she was confident she would never feel ready.

Her whole situation was insane. The plan Lily had helped her hatch was as terrible as it sounded. Trying to protect her, Emma had told Lily in almost every second sentence that she didn't want her to be a part of this, and that helping her get the dress would be the end of Lily's involvement, but Lily wouldn't hear any of it. Like a broken record, Lily repeated the same argument over and over again.

She parroted it once again as they moved further from Antoinette's flat. "This is my chance out as much as it is yours, Emma. I do not desire to be a prostitute for the rest of my life. I want to meet a nice fellow, settle down, have sucklings. This is my last chance to make it out of here."

Just like all the other times, Emma understood what she was saying, but she didn't like making Lily an accomplice.

Lily and Emma split up as Lily said she had a few more things to arrange before the launch of their campaign. Emma's heart was pounding, and her hands were getting sweaty just thinking about it. Emma decided to go over the plan again. She was lost in such deep thought, she didn't even notice when she arrived back at Lily's room. It was already getting dark out when Emma finally noticed that Lily was still not back. How many hours had passed since they split? She was about to get worried when the door opened and Lily entered the dark room that she called home.

"Why are you sitting in the dark?" Lily wondered.

"I wasn't sure how much candles cost, so I didn't want to light one."

Lily laughed at Emma. "Candles are not that expensive. And we shall have more than enough candles soon."

Lily tended to be too easy-going. She reminded Emma a little bit of a Victorian Lisa. No, as sweet and strong as Lily was in certain ways, she was also childish in others. It was all on Emma to lead this insane mission to success — or prison.

Lily handed Emma a piece of hard bread out of her wool bag. Not expecting dinner, Emma accepted it gratefully.

"I was able to get your old blue dress redone into a coat. The shop owner was ecstatic about the material. Said he had never seen a finer, more durable fabric before. I said it was for an American heiress."

"It's called made-in-China polyester."

"Yes, that makes sense. Chinese items are quite expensive and exotic."

Emma almost laughed. *Not where I come from.*

"I also talked to Skip. He will be our carriage driver."

"Can we trust him?"

"Oooooh, yes. I lied for him once and kept his neck out of jail. He stole food for his little sisters after his mother passed. Said he was with me all day in court and got him out, lying under oath."

"Good. So, I guess we have everything to really pull this insane plan off. Technically." Emma shook her head again for the thousandth time in disbelief.

This was crazy.

"Let's go over it again. That friend of yours, Skip, will borrow his friend's carriage for a day. We will drive it out into the country —"

"With me as your lady's maid."

"Yes, with you as my lady's maid. I am a rich heiress from America who hired you and Skip here in London. We were on our way to look at an estate when a group of thieves who never existed to begin with robbed us. Skip will lie and confirm that we were robbed. Did you find out the name of an estate for sale?"

"Yes. The estate agent I spoke to today said there is one for sale close to the Blackwell property. It is called Evergreen Castle. I said an heiress from America wanted to look at it, so if the Duke of Davenport asks around, that is what the estate agent will tell him."

"Splendid. So, we will drive the carriage out near the duke's estate and have him come to my rescue."

"Yes. But this is the part I do not understand. Why not choose some nice, rich fellow who is easy to influence? With your looks and charm, you can choose from plenty of decent rich men. The Duke of Davenport is quite the opposite of decent, and rather cunning. He is a gamble."

This was the part Lily and Emma had disagreed on all week. Emma could not get herself to deceive a nice man into marrying her. It went against her core beliefs as a human being. For years, she had watched her father abuse and cheat on her mother, but instead of using her looks and brains to break every man's heart in revenge, she swore she would never hurt anybody the way her father had hurt her mother. So, no, she would not marry some nice guy for money and then just disappear back into the future and break his heart, making him the laughingstock of society. Emma had asked Lily to name the most notorious womanizer in all of London. She'd asked for a man who thought he was better than everyone else. A man who never felt the slightest bit of love in his heart for a woman.

Lily had answered all three of these requests with the same name—Lord William Blackwell, Duke of Davenport and owner of Blackwell Castle. One of the most entitled, arrogant, and notorious men in all of society. This Duke of Davenport was so famous, every woman in town knew him. Not because he had slept with all of them but because he didn't think any of them were worthy of being with him. He treated servants the same as the ladies of society—with absolutely no respect.

Despite all of that, Emma was more than certain that she could make this Duke of

Davenport marry her. If she wanted to, Emma could make a man believe that he needed her. Not out of love, but out of a want to possess her. Although she'd never used her dark talent, Emma was *the* master of playing games. A despicable skill she'd learned by watching her piece of shit father make women fall for him, again and again, no matter how many times he broke their hearts. A skill Emma never thought she would ever use. Until now.

"So, we stage that robbery near the Blackwell Castle, where Davenport does his daily rides on his horse around noon. I will say that the robbers hit me on my head with a pistol when I refused to give them all of my possessions. There were three, all wearing masks. None of them said anything, as they all only gestured."

Luckily, Emma had just taken a blow to her head, when that car hit her, so that part was true. Emma had told Lily that she wanted to stay as close to the truth as possible. She'd learned that many years ago when dealing with her drunk father. He would believe her as long as the lie was close to the truth. She hated doing it, but in her childhood, it had often made the difference between her mother getting a beating or not.

"And if everything goes according to plan, he will take me in to assist a lady in need and try to help me get back on my feet. I will use this time to make him think that he needs to possess me."

"Not fall in love?" Lily asked, confused.

"No, men like him don't love. They want trophies; they want to possess. I just have to make it clear that possession means a ring on my finger. After that, I will have the money and time I need to find my way back home."

Lily seemed to have mixed feelings about this part too. Emma noticed it immediately.

"What is it?"

Lily fetched a comb and a few decorative pins out of her bag and waved Emma to sit down next to her on the floor.

"You know that there are certain things in a marriage that happen between a man and a woman," Lily said in a tone appropriate for a fifteen-year-old who'd never been kissed by a boy before.

Emma sat down next to Lily, who started brushing her hair.

"Lily, this might come as a shock to you, but I am not a virgin."

Lily stopped brushing her hair for a second.

"So, you are not a lady in waiting where you come from?"

Emma laughed wholeheartedly. Even in terrible times like these, Lily was able to make her laugh.

"No, Lily. I'm not. Where I come from, men and women can be romantic with each other before marriage. It's totally normal and widely practiced."

Lily leaned sideways next to Emma to be able to see her face.

"Are you certain? And that is deemed as acceptable?"

Emma felt a little bit of pride for her time and how far women's rights had come. Sure, sexism was still a very real thing, but women didn't have to prostitute themselves out seven days a week for a piece of hard bread and an empty studio. At least not in most parts of the world.

"It is, yes. Women can have as many relationships as they want to before they settle on someone they think worthy of marriage."

"That sounds incredible. I wish I could reside where you are from," Lily said in a tone of sadness.

Emma was not a virgin, but she was also not someone who would have sex with just anybody, especially not for wealth. That was totally new territory for her, and even if the Duke of Davenport was a real ass, she still felt terrible about the whole thing. But what else was she supposed to do? She'd played with the idea of being a high-class prostitute, but now it wasn't just her own life she had to think about. It was Lily's as well. Lily had done so much for her. She'd saved her life, for heaven's sake. How could she let her down? She was so hopeful that this would work and land her a job at an estate as a lady's maid, away from the constant fear of abusive customers. Emma couldn't even imagine the bunch of sickos Lily had to do business with.

Emma looked at Lily's reflection in the window. She held a hair pin in her hand like it was part of a mathematical equation before remembering what to do with it. She tucked it under Emma's hair on the side of her head.

"Ouch!" Emma cried out in protest.

"Sorry. I shall be more careful. It has been a while."

Great. She worried that Lily's experience as a lady's maid was a bit of an overstatement and that this might turn into a painful night. Then there was still that elegant green dress that Emma had to put on. Late Victorian fashion was stunning, sure. Dresses were more comfortable in 1880 than those Queen Elizabeth movie dresses. As the Victorian era was sort of the start of women being allowed to be more active in their daily lives, it also made dresses more wearable, while at the same time dragging an elegant tail in the back. Still, there was that horrible hourglass corset that Emma was not looking forward to.

Out of nowhere, her new lady's maid got serious. "Emma?" Lily put the brush and pins aside and walked around to face her.

"Yes?"

"When you figure it out, I mean how to go back home... Can I come with you?"

Emma hadn't expected the question. But why the hell not? Lily lived in the equivalent of female hell.

"I can only imagine what it would be like to go to university and be with a man for love."

Lily's words broke Emma's heart. How could Emma deny her those things? The fundamental rights of every woman? Emma stood up and grabbed Lily's hands as a gesture of her deepest sympathy.

"I promise you, from the bottom of my heart, I will do whatever I can to take you with me."

Lily threw her arms around Emma's neck.

"Thank you. I do not know how to ever repay you," Lily cried, holding on to Emma as if her life depended on it—which, it kinda did. Emma lovingly wiggled herself out of Lily's firm, slightly choking grip.

"You don't have to thank me. You saved my life, too, remember? We better get going."

Lily nodded and an expression of hope and happiness lit up her face.

"Can I get a box like yours when we get there?"

"Sure, but first, we have to make me look like a lady, open the wound on my head again, fake a robbery, get the duke to marry me, and then find a way back home."

"It's my pleasure."

They both laughed like they had been best friends all their lives.

CHAPTER 4

Neither Emma nor Lily were able to rest even for a minute that night.

Lily seemed to have forgotten how to put on a lady's dress and how to make up Emma's hair, so it took them hours just to get Emma ready the next morning. Emma had never felt so lost without Google before, which prompted Lily to ask if Mr. Google was an all-knowing scholar.

They also went over the plan again and did some fine-tuning. Emma added that they should cut the horses loose and say that the thieves did it to avoid being followed. Surely the Duke of Davenport would help get them back to Skip. Lily also taught Emma everything she knew about being a lady, which honestly wasn't much. Emma wasn't too worried, as she had seen countless period movies with her mother, so she knew a few things about the respectable behavior of ladies. And then there was also the good ol' "Sorry, I'm American." Lily said that the British pictured Americans as some sort of wildlings shooting pistols into the air while riding horses over oil-rich fields.

Fair enough. That would help her get away with a lot.

It was barely light out when Skip arrived. Emma couldn't believe it. There he was. With a carriage. It was an older model and out of fashion, but it would do the job. Lily gave Emma a powerful pat on her shoulder, which made her stumble forward a bit.

"Told you not to worry about Skip. He is one of us."

Skip was a tall, skinny redhead, barely older than twenty. He was sitting on the driver's bench in front of the carriage and was dressed the part but still looked kind of misplaced, like he was only a temporary carriage driver.

"Howdy!" Skip removed his hat with a cheeky smile, turning it into a jolly greeting. Emma offered her hand for a handshake but withdrew it right away. Shoot. She and Lily had talked about this. Ladies did not greet servants with handshakes. In fact, handshakes were uncommon for ladies with anybody. She knew that but was so used to handshakes, this would undoubtedly happen again.

"Nice to meet you, Skip. Thanks for doing this. It would also be just fine if you'd rather not get involved. No hurt feelings."

"Oh, please! I'm glad I can finally pay Lily back for wot she's done for me and me sisters," he said in a strong Cockney accent.

He helped Emma into the carriage and took a few steps back to get a better look at her.

"By God, yer did not tell me that she was the prettiest girl in all of England, Lily!"

"I did not want to give you false hope. Your pockets are as empty as they are old, and a good heart is not going to get us out of here," Lily teased him.

Indeed, Emma looked nothing short of stunning. Even without the jewelry that she traded for the green dress, she felt confident she could easily pass for a true lady. It had taken Lily hours, but she'd managed to turn Emma from a twenty-first-century student into a period princess. The dress looked like it was made for her. The green silk matched her eyes perfectly, and her strawberry-blonde hair, which Lily had fashioned into an elegant bun, made her eyes and dress stand out even more.

Skip shook his head and closed the carriage door. "Remember, Lily, the lady has to get in and out of the carriage first," he reminded her. Lily had gotten in first, a grave transgression for a lady's maid.

"Oh, bloody hell. Of course..."

Skip nodded his head and took his seat on the front bench of the carriage behind the horses. He gave the horses a signal that sounded like a whistle, and off they went in a steady but fast clip.

Emma took a deep breath, in and out, but met with some resistance from the cruel corset cinching her ribs to her spine. There was no turning back now. This was it. Her heart pounded against her chest like it wanted to escape. Lily, on the other hand, seemed surprisingly relaxed and cheerful, but that was the innocent, child-like character Lily was able to maintain despite her horrendous line of work.

The ride to the Blackwell property was only going to take two to three hours, so they decided they would stop somewhere to go over the plan with Skip again—for the millionth time.

They found a nice spot behind a tree line, right where the duke would do his daily rounds on his famous black stallion, Thunder. This was public information. Davenport was a hot commodity and had a regular spot in the usual gossip sheets of society. It was well known that he was a passionate horseman who also loved to stick to his schedule and his schedule alone. To the minute.

Great, I will not only be marrying a prick but a prick with OCD. Emma tried to stay positive, telling herself that she would get out of here in no time anyway, so she might not even have to stay married to this duke for very long. She and Lily would just disappear into thin air and wake up in the twenty-first century before the year was over.

"It's time," Skip announced, looking at his pocket watch. He got out of the carriage and back on the bench. The horses started moving again. Emma directed her nervous gaze at Lily.

"It will be fine," Lily said. "Just be yourself. With all your education and wit, they won't doubt that you are a lady. I never thought anything else of you from the minute I saw you passed out on the side of the road."

Lily's words did make Emma feel better. Then the carriage stopped abruptly, shaking Emma and Lily in their seats. Oh God! It was really happening! Emma leaned out the window and watched Skip jump off the carriage to cut the horses loose, but the horses didn't move an inch.

"Bloody hell." He took off his coat and swung it wildly into the air to scare them.

Much to Emma's relief, it did the trick, and the horses launched in different directions, one down the road, the other over a field. Skip then surveyed the area anxiously, something Emma did as well, to make sure nobody had seen him. Nobody was in sight. This was it. Emma's only chance to get her and Lily out of female hell.

Lily seemed to hear every word of Emma's encouraging thoughts out loud, using this moment of determination to swing the carriage door open and jump out onto the street to join Skip. They whispered to each other, but Emma was too far to hear what they were talking about. Suddenly, they both stared in the same direction. Lily turned around and gave Emma a hectic sign to move backward, deeper into the carriage, out of sight. Wait? Was somebody coming?

Yes! Emma heard horses and voices. *Jesus. Somebody's coming!* Emma scratched the scab off her head wound. Blood came running down her face. Not like a river, but enough to make it noticeable. A feeling of shame overcame her, spreading through her body and into her throat to form a lump that threatened to choke any attempted sound. She felt like a total fraud. What the hell was she doing here? She had to remind herself again and again that this was the only way out. She needed to get back home, taking poor Lily with her, and that ruthless Duke of Davenport was her ticket out.

Emma heard a man's voice, but she couldn't understand what was being said. Why the hell was Lily not playing her part? She was supposed to yell at the duke for help. Were they already discovered at the very first stage of the whole plan? Were English Victorian prisons as bad as American ones? Could she choose to be sent to the colonies? Were there colonies? Emma's head was spinning. She started to feel nauseous.

Get it together! Take a deep breath! Deep breath! Get it together. Suddenly, the voices got louder and more frantic.

"What is going on? Is anybody hurt?" a man's voice shouted like thunder in the clouds.

Emma saw Lily rushing toward the carriage door. She opened her mouth to say something, but before she could even get a word out, a man pushed her aside. His tall stature blocked the whole door as he leaned into the carriage. He was lean and wore an elegant black day suit that fit him like it was hand-tailored, which it probably was. His face had a noble handsomeness to it. His neatly combed brown hair matched his beautiful brown eyes perfectly, which hypnotized Emma for a moment. She could never have dreamt that the Duke of Davenport would have such warm, beautiful, kind-looking eyes. She was truly amazed by the sheer grace of the man.

Emma glanced over to Lily, whose head was shaking a strong no from behind the man's shoulder.

The man seemed to study Emma for a second, gazing from her face to her head wound. Slowly, like he would approach a wounded animal, he took a step into the carriage.

"Do not be scared. It looks like you are hurt. May I assist you out of the carriage to examine your wound in the light?"

Still hypnotized by the man, Emma nodded a soft yes to him. Where the hell was her voice? She scolded herself silently, *Say something!*

The man gently took Emma's left hand to help her up on her feet. He then placed his other hand around her waist to get a steady grip on her so she wouldn't fall on her way out of the carriage. His touch made her shiver but in a weird, warm way.

He noticed her shiver but mistook it for fear. "Do not worry. I shan't hurt you. I promise. You are safe now," he said in that calming, beautiful voice of his.

Beautiful voice? When had she ever noticed a man's voice to be beautiful? She tried to step out of the carriage, but the small doorway forced her to briefly press against her rescuer's chest and stomach. Her whole body erupted in tingly shockwaves. This man was nothing but lean muscle. It must have been all those years without the touch of a man that made her react so strongly to this one. Or, at least that's what she told herself.

The man walked Emma slowly toward a spot under a tree a few feet away from the carriage. Lily and Skip stared at the whole scene like bystanders at an accident. Skip was holding one of the horses that had run off and another horse that appeared to belong to the gentleman. It was a pretty white horse, but it surely did not look like the world-famous "Thunder" to Emma. The man took off his coat and laid it on the ground under the tree for Emma to sit on. The sky was cloudy and looked like it could rain at any moment.

"Here, please sit down. I need to touch your head now to look at the wound."

Emma sat down and leaned her head sideways to give him better access to the wound.

"What happened?" the man directed his question toward Lily and Skip, who appeared to be frozen like they were ice sculptures.

What was the matter with them? It took a second, but Skip finally took a step forward. "Robbed. We...we were robbed."

The man gently tilted Emma's head a bit more and split her hair to the side where the wound was located.

"It is not too deep. Do you know what year it is?"

Emma almost smiled because this was such a ridiculous situation. After time traveling and faking a robbery, she was asked what year it was! Still, she answered, "1881."

"Good. I do not think it is serious, but we must get you out of the cold and have you seen by a doctor immediately." It was almost as if the man had given Lily her cue, and she finally found her acting talents again.

"They took everything! The Mrs. refused to give them her trunks and her purse, so they hit her on the head with a pistol," Lily said hysterically, throwing her head into her hands in despair. "We were all so scared for the Mrs., but we could not get help because they cut the horses loose. I thought she would die!"

Was Lily crying? Wow, she was really putting her heart into this masterpiece of a theater act. Even Skip, who was in on it, seemed to be taken by her performance and looked at Lily as if he wanted to comfort her.

Suddenly, another carriage arrived, and two women came launching out of it like their carriage was on fire. One of them was an older, heavier lady who had a motherly aura about her. She was clearly wearing too much makeup, and her dress was so colorful it almost hurt Emma's eyes. The other one was on the heavier side as well but was young and plain looking. There was no doubt they were mother and daughter. They both came running toward Emma.

"Oh Lord, Lord, LORD, WHYYYY!?" shouted the older one frantically, throwing her hands up to the sky as if she were talking to God in person. The younger one grabbed her mother by the arm and held a tissue to her face.

"Look how beautiful she is! How can the Lord let something terrible happen to an angel like this?" She started crying. Emma, Lily, and Skip exchanged confused looks. The good-looking man, however, turned around and looked lovingly at the two women, who were more emotional than the supposedly robbed Lily and Emma.

"It will be all right, Agnes. How about you take Mother back to the carriage, and make some room for the lady? She needs our help now."

Mother? How could this man be related to those two? He was everything period dramas always tried to make a true gentleman look like. But then, Emma wasn't judging people by their looks. And the fact that they instantly ran back to the carriage to help showed Emma that they were annoying but kind people. Emma glanced at the man again; he was kneeling right in front of her. He was nothing like Lily had described. Emma had expected a monster, but Davenport was helpful and had the kindest eyes she had ever seen. He was very handsome, in face and form, and exuded a self-assuredness that drew her to him further.

All of a sudden, her rescuer jumped up and placed his impressive stature in front of Emma, as though he was ready to fight the returning robbers with nothing more than his fists and his sheer will. There were three men approaching on horses—fast. Like the cavalry, they came riding toward the group, making the ground shake underneath them. One horse was faster than the others and got to Emma and the rest of the group before the other two did. The man who was on top of this beautiful, black warhorse brought it to an abrupt standstill that covered Lily and Skip in a cloud of road dust. They both started coughing, waving the dust away from their eyes. He dismounted the black beast in one fluid motion and came running toward Emma.

"Out of the way, Evergreen!" the imposing man said, his voice deep and commanding as he pushed Emma's rescuer out of the way—who let it happen without a fight. Though obviously annoyed, he deferred to the new arrival, his nod indicating he knew the rude man.

"Evergreen?" Emma asked in confusion.

"Oh, my goodness! Davenport! Thank the Lord!" shouted the older lady from her carriage. Her daughter followed suit. "Your Grace! I am so relieved you came to our rescue!"

Emma saw Lily giving her a hasty nod that confirmed what she was slowly beginning to grasp.

"You…you are the Duke of Davenport?" she asked the man now kneeling in front of her, who did a quick scan of the wound on her head.

"I certainly am. William Blackwell, Duke of Davenport, at your service, my lady."

Things were starting to make sense now. Her first rescuer was not the Duke of Davenport. He was a lord called Evergreen. That's why Lily and Skip had appeared so confused when he came to Emma's rescue.

Yes, there was no doubt that the man in front of her was clearly the notorious Davenport. He was probably the most attractive man Emma had ever seen in her life. He was nothing but muscles under his silky black suit; which made Evergreen's coat look like yesterday's fashion. His hair was as black as the night and his eyes as blue and clear as a winter storm. If this had still been the twenty-first century, the duke would have been a movie star or an A-list model. No doubt. For some reason, Emma started to regain the confidence that Lord Evergreen had somehow held hostage with his hypnotizing brown eyes and sincere kindness.

The duke turned around to his companions, who, by the looks of their uniforms, must have been his servants. "Now, do not just sit there idle on my horses! You! Ride into town to get the doctor! And you! Ride ahead to my estate and give notice that we are on our way and need the red room to be prepared for an injured guest!"

The two servants immediately rode off in different directions like their jobs depended on it.

"Evergreen, tell your mother and sister to make room in your carriage so we can move the injured lady to my estate."

Emma looked at Evergreen, who didn't say a word but clearly analyzed the situation with cool eagle eyes. His mother and sister, on the other hand, made way to their own carriage immediately. Even Lily and Skip moved out of the way for Davenport, although they weren't even in his path. Clearly, he was used to giving orders and expected them to be followed to his liking.

This was Emma's chance to let Davenport know right then and there that she would be an uphill battle, not a maid in need. Men like the duke and her father loved nothing more than a woman who would be a trophy—not a freebie.

"No," Emma said in a calm but determined voice.

Everybody turned around at the same time, making Emma the centerstage. Davenport looked like it was the first time he'd heard the word "no" in his life—ever.

"Pardon me?" Davenport appeared so confused, he barely got the words out.

"We can tend to my wounds and hurt pride later; they are not fatal. I would rather try to follow the robbers. Not only did they hurt my pride, but they also took off with everything I brought from across the ocean. Time is of the essence now, so let's not waste it." Emma played up her American accent a bit.

And there it was. Davenport truly looked at her for the first time. He had glanced at her earlier, of course, but now he really saw her. He seemed speechless. Everybody was speechless.

"Mrs...?"

"Mrs. Washington. Emma Washington."

Evergreen walked by William and stopped right in front of her. Probably closer than appropriate under normal circumstances, but this situation was unusual for everybody, so nobody seemed to even notice.

"Evergreen. John Evergreen. It is my pleasure to make your acquaintance." He combined a charming smile with an elegant bow.

My gosh, this man can smile. It warmed Emma's heart like no smile ever had before.

"Mrs. Washington, I truly admire your strength and bravery. However, you are injured, and it would cause me and my family grave worry if we could not get you seen by the doctor as soon as possible. I promise you, we shall chase those robbers to the end of this earth, if need be. But now we need to get you somewhere warm and safe."

"Lord Evergreen has a valid point," Lily chipped in, grabbing Emma's hand. *She should have been an actress.*

"I promise you, we shall not rest until we find the thieves. Until then, you will be safe in our care." John made a gesture toward his family, who still stayed clear of their own carriage like

William Blackwell's earlier command was the law around here.

"Yes. Of course," Emma responded.

Too much arguing could annoy William, so she had to balance her performance of a free-spirited American woman and a reasonable lady well.

Before Emma could get another word out, William literally swept her off her feet. She didn't protest but looked over William's shoulder to get a quick glance at John, who did not seem to like any of this but decided to let it slide.

William's chest was as hard as steel. Emma could literally feel his muscles where her body touched his. He acted like he was carrying a small kitten, her weight and gown of little consequence to his bulging biceps. However, her body didn't react in any way when they touched; she felt absolutely nothing.

Gently, William put Emma inside the carriage, which looked a hell of a lot nicer than the one in which she was supposedly robbed. The fabrics were soft silk, and it had skillfully crafted decorations on the inside. William grabbed Emma's hand and gave it a light squeeze.

"I shall meet you at my estate shortly. And do not worry, I shall not rest until I find those men and see that they receive the worst possible punishment for this cowardly crime."

Emma noticed a spark of anger in his eyes. He seemed to mean what he had said about the robbers, and something told Emma that he would indeed not rest until the robbers were found. Which, in this case, would be never—and could possibly expose Emma's plot.

"Thank you, Your Grace," Emma forced herself to say. William didn't bother to help any of the other women into the carriage. Instead, he swung himself back onto his impressive warhorse like it was a little pony.

"I trust you will deliver her safely, Evergreen. I shall do a quick round to see if I can find any trace of the robbers while their tracks are still fresh." Those were the last words of her intended future husband before he made the ground shake under the feet of Thunder and disappeared down the road.

Evergreen watched Davenport ride off into the unknown as if he'd just finished watching the last act of a theater comedy. He had that dangerously attractive smile on his face again. He then came over to the carriage to help his mother, sister, and Lily into the carriage.

"Mrs. Washington, please do not think badly of me, but I shall now direct the carriage driver to take you and my family back to Evergreen Castle."

"But didn't the duke—" his sister protested, but John interrupted her.

"The Duke of Davenport forgot that his mother and sister are both in London for the season…"

"Ooooohhhhhh," mother and daughter responded simultaneously.

Why was that a problem? Emma was about to ask, but Lily quickly intercepted her.

"How very considerate of you, Lord Evergreen."

She decided to trust Lily on this one.

"Thank you, Lord Evergreen," Emma replied in a sincere tone.

"Mother, Sister…please remember that Mrs. Washington is very tired and would like to rest. I am sure we shall get to know her better sooner than later, but now is not the time for questions and excitement."

"Yes, of course…" Lady Evergreen and her daughter Agnes both made long faces as if they'd been caught with their hands in the cookie jar. Both agreed with silent, disappointed nods. John gave the carriage a slap on its side, which seemed to mean "go" in Victorian carriage language, as the carriage took off immediately.

John exchanged a quick word with Skip, then took his place riding alongside the carriage, like the escort of a princess. His elegance seemed to have skipped his mother and sister, Emma mused, trying to avoid eye contact with the Evergreen ladies. Both of them stared at Emma in what could only be described as pure excitement and anticipation for what was to come. She told herself to be grateful toward them and endure all the questions and annoyance they might bring. In the end, they had agreed to help her just as much as John Evergreen had, and that was a kind thing to do.

Emma looked out the small carriage window onto a gray English countryside. It started to rain, which made Emma thankful for having a roof over her head—at least for a little while. Was this really it? Was it that easy? She still had to win

William Blackwell over completely, but he was already taken with her, or he wouldn't have insisted on taking her to his estate. Interestingly enough, William scared her the least out of the whole mess she'd gotten herself into. She knew that sort of man better than she knew herself. Didn't that mean that everything was going fantastic? Not really.

While the carriage took Emma on a romantic English countryside ride, her thoughts were heavily occupied with the very thing she had successfully managed to avoid her whole life—a man. And it wasn't the ridiculously handsome, rich, and muscular William Blackwell, Duke of Davenport.

CHAPTER 5

John rode his horse like the devil was after him. He didn't leave the carriage out of sight even for a minute, until they arrived on his lands and he started to see farmers and servants going about their usual business. They would be safe from here on, so he decided to ride ahead to make the necessary preparations. John wanted to make sure that Mrs. Washington's room was ready and the doctor waiting in it before she arrived. The doctor was actually an employee of his, and the room would be ready in no time, considering how clean his mother kept the estate at all times.

So why was he so beside himself? Sure, today's events were more than unfortunate, especially for poor Mrs. Washington, but John had seen so much worse. It made no sense to be so emotional about Mrs. Washington's incident. He had been to war in the Far East not once but twice, and his charity work with lost veterans was more of a nightmare than a beautiful tale of love and kindness. Most of the veterans he worked with were beyond the trouble of alcoholism. Just last week, he was almost stabbed to death by Milly, a war veteran not much older than John himself, after John found him passed out in the streets. Milly had been having a nightmare about the war. When John woke him, he thought he was the enemy and swung his knife at him, leaving a deep wound on John's lower arm.

So, what was it that angered — no, *enraged* — him so when he thought of someone hurting Mrs. Washington? Obviously, she wasn't dying, unlike the many women and children he had witnessed in the Far East during his deployment. It had been a common sight for his troops — peaceful villages destroyed by the enemy to prevent them from providing John's troops with supplies. The sight of it had been nothing short of unimaginable horror.

So, what was it about this woman? It couldn't be her beautiful green eyes or her noble face, the fact that she looked like she'd just stepped out of a DaVinci painting. John was never a man who paid much attention to looks. Had he become shallow in a matter of minutes thanks to Mrs. Washington?

No, there was something else about her. She had a kind and selfless sparkle in her eyes that had captivated John from the moment he looked into them, long before he even noticed her beauty. Those were the eyes of a woman who would give her life without a second thought for the people she loved.

John didn't have to yell for servants when he arrived at the estate. The way he rode his horse up to the house forced servants to shout and come running on their own.

"Send for Ackley. An injured guest is arriving any minute. And prepare a room for our guest. Make sure it is in the family wing, on the same floor as my mother's and my own."

Who knew—maybe those robbers knew Mrs. Washington from somewhere and would come back for her. Perhaps she was in trouble. She was certainly headstrong, and that could leave angry people behind. Davenport would soon be one of them when he noticed that Mrs. Washington was not at his estate when he returned. Although, in all fairness, Davenport would be more upset with him than with the injured, beautiful Mrs. Washington. He couldn't help but feel a bit of joy over that. It was not in his nature to rejoice over others' unhappiness. Still, in the deepest corner of his heart, John had not yet forgiven Davenport for what he did to him all those years ago. Upsetting him was nothing John would fret over. Quite the opposite.

"And send a messenger to the duke to tell him that Mrs. Washington is in the care of Lady Evergreen and her daughter."

John dismounted his horse and gave the reins to a servant, who took it to the stables. Servants were moving around in panic like ants preparing for battle.

"My lord, you have called for me?" Ackley asked, concern written all over his old face.

Ackley was a one-legged, older veteran whom John had picked up out of the gutters of London's worst quarter right after his first tour. He tended to blame Ackley for inspiring his little charity business of saving veterans whenever he returned from a trying night helping those forgotten souls. John did it in a joking manner, but there was some truth in it, as the whole saving-the-veterans thing had started with Ackley. A former army doctor, Ackley had lost his position and rank, as well as everything else, when he began drinking heavily to cope with the horrors of war.

"Yes, thank you for coming so quickly. Please prepare everything you may need to examine a lady with a head injury. We came across a robbery on our way home, and the lady was injured."

"Dear God! Right away!" Ackley disappeared into the horse stables, where he lived in a small flat that came with employment at John's estate.

Just when John started to get worried about why the carriage was not in sight yet, it turned the corner and came down the long driveway. John's heart made a little jump, and a feeling of excitement overcame him at the thought of seeing Mrs. Washington again. Dear God, what the hell was the matter with him? He had only just left her side a few moments ago. He was acting like a teenage boy in love for the first time.

The carriage pulled up, and John nudged the footman out of the way to open the door himself. He felt instantaneous relief when he saw Mrs. Washington sitting in the carriage with the rest of his family. *Where else would she be?* John scolded himself, finding himself exasperated for being so obsessed with their guest. He reached out to grab her hand and help her out of the carriage.

"Mrs. Washington, I have a room prepared for you. The doctor should already be waiting there."

Emma looked at him with relief in her eyes. John froze for a brief moment, marveling at their beauty. He could stare into them all day long.

"Thank you. I am so very grateful for your help. All of your help," Emma said, turning to the Evergreen ladies to make certain they understood that her gratitude was just as much for them as for John.

It was obvious how much that meant to his mother and sister. They both lit up like evening stars. It triggered a warm feeling around his heart to see them so happy. Not many people treated his mother and sister kindly or with respect. He hated society for how they looked down on them simply because they were a little quirky. They both were kind and giving people, but those were attributes society could not care less about. In society, it was all about status, looks, and money. For Emma to be so kind to his mother and sister proved to him that the kindness he saw in her eyes was real. She was so different from the usual pretty ladies John had encountered before. But then, she was American, and they did things differently over there.

"I shall take you to your room. Mother, would you please accompany us?"

"Of course!" Lady Evergreen jostled through Lily and her daughter, excited to be of use.

John wrapped his arm around Emma's waist to help her walk. She didn't protest, and he took it as a sign that she agreed it would be better if he helped her up the stairs.

He could feel the warmth of her body under his hand and couldn't help but catch a quick glimpse of her pink, full lips. He wondered what those beautiful lips would feel like if he kissed them...gently, so they would barely touch. He thought of his lips against her neck while tightly pressing her soft body against his. Suddenly, he felt a wave of ecstatic heat rush through his body. It felt similar to what he felt shortly before battle, just in a different way. A very pleasant way. An arousing way.

"John!" his mother said in a firm, loud tone that tore him from his thoughts.

He realized that they had already arrived in Mrs. Washington's room. He had been so distracted by his arousing thoughts, he hadn't even noticed when they arrived. Everybody was staring at him, most likely wondering why he was still holding Emma's hand and gripping her around her waist.

Holding her fist up to her mouth, Agnes cleared her throat to signal John to release her.

"We shall give the doctor and Mrs. Washington some privacy now," his mother said, probably for the second or third time.

"Yes…yes, of course. My apologies." John immediately let go of Emma.

How embarrassing! What the bloody hell was he doing? He turned around and left the room, followed by his mother and Agnes. He tried to catch a last glimpse of her through the doorway, but Ackley had already closed the door behind them.

Emma looked around the room. It was the most beautiful room she had ever stepped foot in. The walls were decorated with fine silk wallpaper, and everything had a light-blue theme to it. The fireplace was made of solid marble and had a huge oil painting of Evergreen Castle over it. The walls, the bed, the covers, the golden chairs—everything was simply *beautiful*. Exactly like in those period movies Emma's mother used to watch all the time. Her room even had a little vanity with a mirror on it. What a dream! She and Lily had barely been able to catch their breaths the moment they turned onto the alley that led to Evergreen Castle, which stood there looking grand and noble, even in the gloomy rain.

Emma was simply speechless. It didn't help that John Evergreen had walked her through all of this glamour with his arm tight around her waist. There was a moment on the stairs when Emma could have sworn she caught him staring at her lips. If this were the twenty-first century, she would totally have asked John out on a date. Right then and there. Emma felt extremely attracted to him. She had been with men before and was familiar with the feeling of sexual attraction, but there was something else going on here. Her twenty-first-century analytical mind knew exactly what it was. She liked him a lot, which was crazy, considering she had literally just met this man. But how else could she interpret that tingly feeling she felt when he touched her? Sure, she had felt attracted to men before, but this, no…this was no feeling of attraction alone.

Great. Things are already starting to go wrong.

"Please sit down, Mrs. Washington," Ackley instructed Emma kindly.

Emma was trying to not pay attention to his wooden leg, but Lily didn't show that kind of consideration. Ackley noticed her stare.

"Ah, yes, that. Lost in the African war. But that is not a story suited for a lady and her maid."

Lily seemed embarrassed for staring now and looked away. He noticed that as well.

"No need to feel embarrassed. I am far used to the looks. They are part of my life now. But that is enough talk about an old fool like me. What brought you all the way over here?" Ackley asked as he gently brushed Emma's hair aside to look at her head wound. He then turned to Lily and said, "Would you be so kind as to hand me that bag over there?" He pointed to his bag on the wooden coffee table.

Lily fetched it for him.

"Now, this will sting a little." He put some clear liquid on a piece of white cloth and held it on Emma's head wound.

It burned like hell, but Emma didn't even flinch. Thanks to her father, she was well accustomed to the burning of alcohol on wounds. He was too cheap to spend three bucks on hydrogen peroxide and used his liquor instead.

One time, Emma fell off her bicycle and came running into the house with wounds on her arms and knees. Daddy hadn't even gotten up from the couch; he grabbed his liquor from the coffee table and just poured it onto Emma's arm straight out of the bottle. Then he handed her the bottle to do her knees herself.

"I see you American ladies are not only brave but also pretty tough when it comes to pain." Ackley smiled at her warmly in reference to her attempt to chase the robbers.

How was that even possible? One of the Evergreen ladies had to have already told the servants about the incident before they even reached the room. Fair enough, she could use their love for gossip to her advantage, now that she knew of it.

"Mrs. Washington is truly amazing, isn't she?" Lily said in overly dramatic admiration. It was probably an attempt to create a good picture of Emma in front of Ackley, who would most likely report to John Evergreen later on.

"I could not agree more. Here, hold that down for a few minutes." Ackley grabbed Emma's hand and pressed it against the cloth on her wound. "I do not see any symptoms of head trauma. It is more of a superficial scratch. Did those cowards hurt you anywhere else?"

Emma shook her head.

"Good. It would be better to rest for the next few days. I can only imagine how disturbing the whole thing must have been for you, and we do not want you to suffer from mental trauma."

Emma felt ashamed again for faking the robbery, but then, she did get hit by a car and woke up in Victorian England, so there was certainly fodder for mental trauma.

Ackley put his things away and sat down on the golden couch next to one of the two big windows. "Did you see what the robbers looked like?"

"They were all wearing the same outfits. All black," said Lily.

"Did they say anything? Did they have an accent?"

"No," Emma responded in a manner that sounded apologetic for not having more valuable information.

"They took everything. The lady's clothes, money, jewelry—it is all gone. What are we supposed to do now?" Lily sounded desperate.

"Don't worry. Your lady is in good hands now, I promise. The Evergreens are wonderful people and will take good care of you for as long as it is needed. In the meantime, we shall do everything we can to find those criminals and return your belongings to you."

"I don't know how to thank you all."

"Oh, please, it is our duty to help others. If I may ask, what were you doing out here?"

"I'm trying to establish roots in Europe and wanted to look at Evergreen Castle, but there must have been a mistake. I was informed that it was for sale?"

"Well, it is not any of my business, but you are correct about that. The master listed it for sale many years ago but turns down every offer he receives. And there have been quite a few, if I may say so. I do not know why those agents even still list it."

"Why did he list it for sale but has never accepted any offers on it?" Emma asked curiously.

"That is something you would have to ask the master. It is not my estate, so it is not for me to say."

"Of course."

What an honorable, faithful servant Ackley was. If that was even the right word to describe his position here. He seemed to be more than just that to the kind family who lived here. Emma wanted to talk to him about the medicine and the use of pharmacies in Victorian England, but that would have to wait. For now, she was more than happy that 1881 seemed to know about the importance of disinfecting wounds. Infections had killed more people in this era than cancer and war combined.

"Well, I shall let you rest now."

He gathered his things and opened the door but turned around one last time. "If you need anything, and I mean *anything*, just ask for Ackley."

What a kind man. Emma really appreciated it. "Thank you. I will."

Ackley nodded in satisfaction and closed the door behind him. Emma and Lily waited for a few seconds, listening to his footsteps disappear in the distance before Lily came running to Emma, who was still sitting on the chair next to the fireplace.

"This is going better than I could have ever imagined," Lily whispered joyfully.

"What?" Emma said way too loudly.

Lily tried to cover Emma's mouth with her hand, but Emma swatted her hand away like it was an annoying fly.

"How can you say that? We were supposed to be at the Duke of Davenport's castle. Not here! The whole thing is not going according to plan at all."

"You cannot be at Davenport's. Not with his family out of town. Without a female invitation or companion, your reputation would be ruined. And I am just a servant; I do not count."

"Ohhh." Lily was right. How could she have forgotten about the whole reputation thing? It was all those novels and movies ever talked about. She had to be more careful to not think every mistake could simply be pushed to the side with the excuse of being American.

"On top of that, did you see the way Lord Evergreen was looking at you?"

"Lily, no. I told you I wouldn't hurt a nice—"

"I know, I know. You shan't hurt a nice man." Lily rolled her eyes. "But Evergreen is so taken with you. It would make things so easy."

"It would. Maybe he is not as nice as he pretends to be?" Was she really hoping now that Evergreen was a jerk so she could marry him instead?

"Evergreen? I do not want to lie to you, Emma. I know him from the brothels."

"WHAT?" Emma shouted.

Lily tried putting her hand on Emma's mouth again, but just like before, Emma removed it—though she got the message and lowered her voice.

"What do you mean, you know him from the brothels?" Emma felt her heart sink like a lost ship on the wide open. Was she so wrong about Evergreen? Was he just another man with a fake smile and a cheating heart? But why did it bother her so much? Just a minute ago, she wanted him to be a jerk, or had at least pretended that she did. Lily studied Emma's facial expression for a second.

"Calm down. Not in the way you think. What I meant is that I do not want to lie to you about him not being a fine fellow. He is one of the finest. I know him from the brothels because he goes looking for his drunken veterans there from time to time. The whores call him the shining knight, and I probably do not have to explain to you why they call him that."

Emma felt relieved. He wasn't like all these other lusting cheaters. But that also meant that she couldn't change her course from Davenport to Evergreen. Her relief turned to disappointment. She would not make a fool out of Evergreen and ruin him for that special woman who was waiting for him out there somewhere. A woman who would not vanish back into the future—or fake robberies.

"One way or the other, Evergreen was a blessing. Even if you do not marry him, it will make things so much easier with Davenport. Do you see? Now they are rivals for your affection. I must say, I did not think you could really pull this off, but you did it, Emma!"

Emma understood every word Lily said loud and clear. Evergreen's involvement made her more of an interest to Davenport and helped her case immensely. But still, the whole thing made her feel awful. Was she supposed to use poor Lord Evergreen now as a steppingstone to the Duke of Davenport?

"Lily, I beg you, please don't use Lord Evergreen for this charade in any way. He is a nice man, and I don't want him to get hurt." Not to mention that Emma had to be careful around Evergreen herself. She felt so attracted to him that if this were the twenty-first century, there was no way she wouldn't make a move on him.

"Emma, I am not asking you to hurt him. We shall just use him a little bit to speed things up with Davenport."

"It doesn't feel right, Lily. This family has been so kind to us. I almost feel like we should just take our lies and the trouble we might cause and leave right now." Maybe that was better than to lose all self-respect for herself. Lily seemed to sense Emma's struggle and lovingly put an arm around her shoulders. It was sincere. She clearly felt for her.

"I know how you feel, Emma. You are a kind soul, but what are we supposed to do if we leave now? Go back to the slums of London to whore around for a piece of bread? Beg at the Duke of Davenport's door to take us in? If we do that, your reputation will be ruined, and he will not be able to ask for your hand in marriage."

Emma hated it, but Lily was right. They had no other choice now but to stay here until Davenport's family returned from London so Emma could stay at Blackwell Castle without losing her reputation.

"You're right. I just don't like how things played out."

"I know, but things happen for a reason, and I am certain that Evergreen has a role in all of this. He will play his part to help us with Davenport. Even if it is just to make the duke worry he could lose you to Evergreen. Men hate that sort of thing."

Emma seemed to have forgotten that it was Lily's job to know what men wanted.

"Very well, but I won't give him false hope or lead him on." Emma had no choice anyway. If she ever wanted to make it back home, she had to follow through with this charade. And now she had Lily to think of as well. She couldn't just send her back to her horrific life as a poor prostitute. She would simply stay away from Lord Evergreen as much as she could. Not only for his sake but for hers as well. She liked him way too much already.

"Do you still have my phone?"

"Yes, it is right here." Lily pulled it out from under her skirt and handed it to Emma.

She stared at it like it was the only connection she had left of her home. Well, it *was* her only connection to home. Everything else, including her purse, Lily had traded for things they needed to make Emma look like a lady. Emma surveyed the room to find a good spot to hide it. After inspecting a few potential places, she decided to put it inside one of the chairs' seat cushions. Even a detailed room cleaning would not reveal her phone in there.

Suddenly, they heard a noise from behind the door that was on the left of Emma's bed. Lily and Emma both froze. Was somebody listening to them? Lily went over to the door and opened it forcefully, but instead of catching a spy, Lily revealed a maid who was pouring water into a bathtub. She stopped in her tracks once she noticed Emma and Lily.

"Excuse me, my lady, I did not mean to disturb you. Lord Evergreen asked me to prepare a hot bath for you, in case you felt like taking one."

Emma wanted to fall to her knees. She had a bathroom! Emma had not showered or bathed since before she got here, well over a week ago. Poverty didn't come with bathtubs. At best, it came with a washbasin and a little cloth. No soap, of course. It was awful. But now, standing in this beautiful bathroom, Emma felt like luck had traveled to late Victorian England with her. Thinking about it, had she traveled just another hundred years back, she would have been in a time period of severe hygienic neglect. People before the nineteenth century had only bathed every other month or so. All those fancy dresses and majestic palaces had been filled with horribly smelly people. God, it had been so bad, people had worn flea traps under their clothes to catch those little suckers in action.

Emma's bathroom even had an early version of a normal toilet. For days, Emma had been using a metal pot as a toilet because she refused to use the wooden bench with a hole in it that was shared by the whole street Lily lived on. Yes, the entire damn street!

No, she would not go back there. She would do whatever was necessary to make it back home—or at least find a way for her and Lily out of poverty.

Thanks to the Evergreens, Emma and the whole time-travel nightmare had turned a hundred and eighty degrees.

She walked over to the bathtub and dipped her hand into the hot, soapy water. This was more of a dream. Emma felt excitement for the first time since she was woken up by the man who tried to rob her a hundred years before she was born.

CHAPTER 6

Emma woke up to noises in the hallway. It sounded like servants going about their business. Rolling over in her sumptuous bed, she went over the last of the previous evening in her head. She must have passed out right after taking a bath. Now, she was absolutely starving. A light snore alerted her that Lily was still sleeping next to her.

"Lily, wake up."

"No refunds, you prick," Lily said, half-asleep.

Emma got out of bed and looked out of one of the ridiculously tall windows. The sun hit the trees and grass like a golden paintbrush, soaking them in warm, glittering light. Evergreen Castle towered beneath a crystal-clear blue sky.

"Just a typical morning in a Victorian castle. Nothing unusual," Emma mumbled sarcastically.

Lily got up and stretched herself. "I have not slept this well in years."

Strangely enough, Emma had to agree with her. She had not slept well since…gosh, never, thanks to her father. Hearing her mother's cries almost every night had resulted in an extremely light sleep pattern, as she had always had to be ready to comfort her. Lily helped Emma dress and put her hair up. She looked stunning in the green dress, even if it looked like it had been through a lot with Emma, which it kinda had.

"I shall go down to the kitchen and see if I can get breakfast there. You should go into the formal breakfast room and join the Evergreens. We shall meet up afterward. I have to do some chores that come with the job of a lady's maid." Lily opened the door for Emma with an energetic smile. Emma stopped at the door.

"I don't feel comfortable with you doing this kind of work for me, Lily."

"You truly are a big softy, aren't you? Always worried about everybody else first." Lily tucked a strand of Emma's hair behind her ear and teased her with a slight bow. "After you, my lady."

Emma teased her back with a deep curtsy of her own, but Lily stopped smiling and looked straight past Emma.

"Good morning, my lord."

Emma jumped up from her curtsy. Lord Evergreen was standing right there in the hallway, watching the whole thing with a smile on his face.

"G-Good morning, Lord Evergreen," Emma stuttered, embarrassed.

"Oh, please, call me John. 'Lord Evergreen' makes me sound so old."

"Only if you call me Emma. 'Mrs. Washington' makes me sound so old," Emma joked.

He laughed and walked over to her. "I do hope that I caught you on your way down for breakfast? May I accompany you?" He held his arm up.

"Yes, how very kind." Emma grabbed his arm, thinking how incredibly cute his laugh was.

"I'm so glad to see you all better."

"Yes. Thank you. I guess all I needed was a bit of rest."

"I hope I did not intrude by having the servants prepare a hot bath for you yesterday."

"Oh, God no! It was absolutely heavenly."

John looked at her as if she had just said something unusual. Was this conversation inappropriate?

"I'm sorry," they said simultaneously.

Emma's cheeks burned. "In America, we talk openly about taking baths."

At the same time, John said, "I should not have started such a topic."

Thankfully, Agnes scouted them from across the hallway, interrupting this awkward moment.

"Mrs. Washington! I am utterly thrilled to see you join us for breakfast!" She came running over and grabbed Emma by the arm. "You will have to tell us all about yourself and the wild, adventurous America!"

"Agnes, do not be so nosy."

Emma smiled. "It's all right. I would love to."

Like every room in this house so far, the breakfast room was incredible. A cozy fire was crackling in the fireplace, and there was a big buffet on a table pushed against the wall.

"How wonderful! Mrs. Washington!" Lady Evergreen shouted, lighting up like a Christmas tree. She was dressed in an extremely colorful dress again, just like yesterday—too much to be considered elegant.

"I am delighted to be sitting next to you." Agnes grabbed a plate, waiting in anticipation to see where Emma would be sitting down.

"Agnes, why not let Emma get her breakfast and sit down first?"

"Emma? Are we on a first-name basis already? How wonderful!" Agnes shouted.

"If you don't mind," Emma responded kindly.

"Absolutely not! I would love nothing more than for us to be friends," Agnes said. Lady Evergreen smiled warmly at her daughter, sharing her happiness in her new friendship.

Emma grabbed a plate and chose a bit of everything. Fruit, bacon, eggs, toast—she was starving. She had literally not had food since that old, dry piece of bread at Lily's room. And prior to that, they'd often skipped breakfast and lunch.

A servant leaned over her shoulder and poured her coffee.

"Thank you," she said to the servant and started on her colossal plate. She tried to eat slowly and elegantly despite wanting to just swallow the whole thing, including the darn plate. It was awfully quiet around the table, and Emma noticed that the Evergreens were staring at her.

John came to her rescue. "I tried to send food up yesterday, but you were already asleep. You must be starving."

Emma slowed down even more.

"How considerate. Thank you." Emma felt as if she was saying "thank you" non-stop. This family was so kind to her. Why couldn't Lord Evergreen be some womanizer like Davenport? She could just marry him and start her studies right here out of Evergreen Castle. The Evergreen ladies would be wonderful in-laws. Sure, they liked to gossip and could be a bit annoying at times, but they were kind and non-judgmental, traits Emma judged people by, rather than their looks or sense of fashion.

"Mrs. Washington, oh please, do tell us what brought you to our old, boring England?" Agnes asked, holding a cup of tea between her hands.

"Well, I was looking into relocating here. A change of scenery."

"Are you married, Mrs. Washington?"

"Mother…please," John growled at her, appearing slightly annoyed.

Emma smiled. "It's all right. I'm widowed." Of course, that wasn't the truth, but Lily had recommended this white lie to work around the whole virgin-before-marriage issue—something Emma was definitely not.

Lady Evergreen seemed to have gotten the information she wanted, as she winked at John in such a blatant manner she might as well have blown a trumpet at him.

"Oh, for heaven's sake…" John rolled his eyes next to a giggling Agnes.

Emma watched the whole interaction with a warm feeling around her heart. What a lovely family. Everything she had ever wanted. Nothing she had ever had.

"Well, fear not, Mrs. Washington, we shall assist you in *any* way possible. Even in the matters of the heart." Lady Evergreen now winked at Emma in the same visible fashion she had at John moments ago.

John shook his head in embarrassment. "I do not even know what to say anymore."

Emma thought about Lady Evergreen's intention to help her get married. They must believe that she was some rich heiress hunting for an Englishman. It was a common thing in these times. Women were expected to make marriage their priority. Technically speaking, marriage was pretty much all there was for a woman at this time. That might actually help Emma in her quest to get married to the Duke of Davenport.

"But, first of all, we shall take you shopping. No eligible woman under my roof will have to endure with only one evening dress, even if she looks as agreeable in it as you do," Lady Evergreen announced.

Emma's eyes grew wide and her cheeks warm. That was too much generosity, and she didn't want to accept this offer. "That is too kind of you, but—"

"No 'but,'" John stepped in. "My mother is right—no lady under this roof has ever spared the Evergreen wallet when it comes to dresses, and we shan't start now." He smiled with that devilishly handsome face of his.

There was no way Emma could say no to that, so she agreed hesitantly. Both Evergreen ladies got up from their chairs and rushed out of the breakfast room in pure excitement.

"Penley!" Lady Evergreen shouted on her way out. "Peeeennnnleeeyyyy!" she screamed again from further away.

"I beg your pardon. Let me tell them that you did not mean right now." John stood up, but Emma grabbed his hand to stop him. He froze and looked at her hand holding his. Their eyes met for a second, releasing those butterflies in Emma's stomach again. She instantly let go of his hand.

"Please don't. I would love to go with them."

"In that case…thank you," John said in a soft, gentle voice.

Just then, Agnes came running in. "Are we going to Evergreen or London?"

"Evergreen. London is too far for Emma; she should still rest," John replied.

Agnes turned around and was gone as fast as she had appeared.

"Evergreen?" Emma asked.

"It is a small town not far from here. My family has been here for a long time, so the town is called after us. But really, it is barely a village. It is nothing to trumpet about."

Emma didn't even have a cobblestone named after her, so yeah, it was a big deal.

"Well, I better get Lily." Emma stood. She was finished anyway.

"You can always take one of our servants too. We have also arranged a room for Lily in the wing with the other servants."

Emma didn't want Lily to be too far from her. She needed her for so many things. Without Lily, her reputation would already have been ruined, as she would have taken Davenport's offer and stayed with him at his castle, not knowing the consequences. But above all, Lily was her friend.

"If you don't mind, I would like to keep Lily close. She comforts me so, and I trust her."

John nodded without hesitation. "That makes sense. I shall let the servants know to put up a bed for her in your room."

This man was by far the kindest she had ever encountered. And to her, he looked his part. His beautiful brown eyes had a warm shine to them that made Emma feel a little tingle every time he looked at her with that genuine smile of his. He came a little closer and reached to her head but stopped before touching it.

"Do you mind if I take a quick look at your wound?"

"No, I appreciate it."

John gently tilted her chin to the side with one hand and examined the wound with his other. Emma looked at his face. It was so close now, she could actually smell him. He smelled of aftershave. Emma couldn't believe how much his scent aroused her.

"It is healing rather nicely. I do not think you will need to endure another round of Ackley's rubbing alcohol on it. It burns like hell if you ask me." He now turned to her and smiled again.

Their faces were far too close, but neither of them moved away. Emma looked at his lips. They looked so soft. She wondered what kind of a kisser he was. Was he gentle? Emma's cheeks started to burn. John carefully lifted her chin toward his, looking deep into her eyes. His lips parted slightly. Was that desire she saw in his gaze? Emma was on fire. She moved her head in a little bit, to welcome his lips on hers.

"The Duke of Davenport!" his mother suddenly shouted from the hallway.

John jumped back a few steps, which left Emma feeling as though he had been torn from her.

Before she could think too hard about that, Agnes swung the door to the breakfast room open as if she was part of Davenport's cavalry. "It is His Grace for Emma!" she shouted.

"Yes, we heard it the first time, when mother shouted like a newspaper boy in the streets of London. Thank you, Agnes," John said sarcastically but in the voice of a perfect gentleman.

For some reason, Emma felt annoyed by Davenport coming here. She honestly couldn't think of anything worse right now than having to spend time with him.

Emma and John joined his mother and Davenport in the tearoom. Like every other room in this house, it was a beautifully decorated room that looked like a scene out of *Downton Abbey*.

Davenport looked stunning, Emma had to give him that. Like John, he was wearing a black day suit with a stand collar, bow tie, and waistcoat, but his was shiny and left the impression that it was made from the finest materials found on this earth. His black hair complemented that face of his, far too good-looking for any human being. His icy blue eyes now locked on her.

"Ms. Washington!" He walked over and gave her that famous slight-bow-hand-kiss combo. "I am so glad to see you in good health. I hope I am not intruding."

Emma was worried for a short moment that John would reply, "*Yes, you were intruding,*" but just like yesterday, John studied Davenport silently with those cold eagle eyes. Was there something the matter between the two of them?

"Thank you for checking in on me and for helping me yesterday."

"Of course. I spent hours yesterday trying to find those thieves, but to no avail. I have hired an investigator, and he will not rest until those cowards are found and brought to justice. The police, I dare say, are rather incompetent when it comes to these matters."

Suddenly, Emma thought of poor Skip. By God, had anybody gone back to help him get the horse back and fix the carriage he had borrowed from his friend? "What about the driver? Skip? He is all right, I hope?"

The duke turned down the corners of his mouth, as if he wanted to ask her why in the name of God she would waste her time worrying about some carriage driver.

"I sent men back yesterday to help him fix the carriage and find the other horse," John told Emma in that caring tone he always used with her.

"What a kind heart you have to worry about such things," Davenport pitched in, sounding totally fake. "Anyway...I hope it is not asking too much of Mrs. Washington to accept this little care package from my family and me."

Davenport signaled Penley to bring something in, but Penley waited for a few seconds to see if John would object, then opened the door to the tearoom to let in several servants carrying boxes of all shapes and forms. Emma hated to admit it, but she was curious about these differently colored and shaped boxes. Agnes ran over to one of the bigger boxes and opened it. She pulled out a beautiful, light-blue silk dress.

"Emma, look at this! It is magnificent!" Agnes squeaked, then opened a round box right next to the one she had just opened to pull out a fancy hat and matching gloves in the same color. Lady Evergreen came over to Agnes to look at the items as well.

"Look at this stitch work. Is that from—"

Davenport smiled smugly. "Wilsons. Of course. My family only frequents the grandest of dressmakers."

Agnes and Lady Evergreen went through box after box like children unwrapping presents on Christmas morning. Emma didn't mind them having fun opening her boxes, and the duke surely enjoyed the big fuss his gifts were getting. Emma glanced at John, who was leaning against the wall watching all of this silently. It was hard to read his face. Was he jealous? As much as it displeased her, she had to thank Davenport, nonetheless.

"Your Grace...I don't know what to say," Emma said honestly.

She really didn't know what to say. She hadn't received a present since she was twelve. Her father had drunk away every cent that ever rolled through their door, and her mother had no money on her own, living off food stamps and housing allowance, unable to ever overcome the trauma Emma's father had inflicted on her.

"Well that puts a fly in the ointment. We shall not get to take Emma shopping now," Agnes sounded disappointed, lowering a purple hat with feathers that she had been holding up against her head.

Emma looked at the sad faces of Lady Evergreen and Agnes, who didn't make any effort to hide their emotions.

"Well, maybe we could try the dresses together. I'm in need of guidance when it comes to the latest British fashion."

Their faces went from rain to sunshine in a matter of seconds, and they both started giggling.

"Well, I am known for my good taste." Lady Evergreen puffed her chest, grinning proudly. "Penley! Where are you?"

Penley walked quietly up to Lady Evergreen like an abused animal. Did he mind hearing his name yelled day in and day out?

"Have these boxes carried to Emma's room immediately!"

Penley did a little courtesy bow and went to go about his duty, but Lady Evergreen grabbed him by his arm, pulling him back abruptly. Penley didn't even flinch and kept the stoic expression that was the mark of a faithful butler fixed on his face.

"And have tea and pastries brought up. Who knows how long this will take," Lady Evergreen babbled in excitement.

Emma turned to Davenport. "Duke, I cannot thank you enough."

"Oh, please. It is the least I can do to help. I wrote to my mother and sister the moment I arrived back at my estate, and they insisted on returning to Blackwell Castle at once. A turn up for the books, don't you think?"

Everybody knew exactly what that meant, between the lines. Emma would now be able to visit and even stay at Davenport's, and although he didn't have to clarify the meaning of their return from London, he still did. "They would be delighted to host you at Blackwell Castle."

This was it. Technically, Emma could pack her bags right then and leave with Davenport to pursue what she had come here to accomplish. But…then why did she try to convince herself it would be better to stay at Evergreen for a little bit longer?

"How kind of you. Maybe a bit later? The doctor recommended rest for a few more days." *What are you doing?* Emma scolded herself inside her head. *You are here on a mission, not a vacation! Fix it! Fix it now!* "But I would be delighted to thank the Duchess of Davenport and your sister in person as soon as I can, if that would work for you?"

Davenport glanced over at John with a smile that had provocation written all over it.

"They would love to make your acquaintance. We are planning a small gathering this Saturday. It would be a true delight to my family and me to have you attend as our guest of honor," Davenport stated, gesturing a servant to bring his coat and hat.

Emma hesitated.

"You and the Evergreens, of course," Davenport added.

"Oh, we would not miss it for anything in the world, right, Emma?" Agnes jumped up and down.

"No...no, we wouldn't," Emma said, analyzing John's expression.

"Saturday, then," were his last words before the magnificent statue of a man left Emma to Agnes and Lady Evergreen, who eagerly dragged her up the stairs to start the fashion show.

Lady Evergreen giggled. "We all have to look our best on Saturday! The Blackwells are the most respectable and well-bred family in all of England."

Emma threw a last glance at John, who watched from the bottom of the stairs with an expression that was hard to read. What was Emma doing? She tried to tell herself that she had just played hard to catch to make Davenport want her even more, but deep down, she knew that there was another reason for wanting to stay at Evergreen just a little longer.

CHAPTER 7

T he days at Evergreen Castle were revealing themselves to be the best of Emma's life. John read every wish from Emma's lips, and Agnes and Lady Evergreen were two of the kindest people Emma had ever met.

In the mornings, they would usually eat breakfast together, followed by a walk through the beautiful Evergreen gardens. Walk by walk, Emma would learn more about them, especially John. He was by far the most amazing man Emma had ever come across—or even heard of. Agnes told Emma that after the death of the former Earl of Evergreen, John's father, John had made some striking reforms to the estate, well ahead of his time. Servants worked on schedules and had two days off a week. They were also paid a fair wage and were free to marry and still maintain their employment at the estate. Children were raised in the servants' quarters, which were generous flats, and John paid for their education.

Agnes also told Emma about John's time in the military, and that he had come back a war hero. Apparently, he now spent most of his free time helping veterans in need. John didn't like it when Agnes glorified him, always telling her to stop and that nobody would be interested in these stories, but Emma was more than curious. She wanted to know everything she could about John Evergreen.

After their walks, Agnes would teach Emma one of the countless "boring" accomplishments a lady was supposed to master before marriage. Agnes never said a bad word when Emma revealed yet another skill she was lacking—pretty much all of them. Quite the opposite. Agnes and Lady Evergreen were beyond thrilled to teach Emma everything an English lady needed to know, from stitching to the most popular songs of the time. In return, Emma taught them everything there was to know about fun activities, from baseball to the card game Apples to Apples, much to the enjoyment of the servants' children, who screamed and squeaked in happiness when Emma played baseball with them or challenged them to another round of Uno using self-made cards.

However, the biggest treat for the Evergreens came in the form of Emma's story time when everybody gathered after dinner in the music room. Even the servants asked for permission to be present during Emma's incredible tales, which ranged from flying machines called airplanes to creating dinosaurs using prehistoric DNA.

"But can the dinosaurs not swim from this island to England when we are asleep?" Timmy, one of the maid's children, asked as he drew his brows together in concern. He was sitting on Emma's lap on the floor next to the fireplace.

"Not if you wash behind your ears and listen to your teachers," Emma said, throwing Tilly, his mother, a cheerful wink.

"I better go do my math then," Timmy said, jumping up from Emma's lap.

"Look at that. I thought you said school is for fools," Tilly said, putting her hands on her hips.

"Mother, please, that was before I learned about the T-Rex." Timmy stormed out of the room, followed by loud laughter. As if it was their cue, the servants started to leave to finish their work before the end of their shifts. John walked over to Emma and helped her back up on her feet.

"What an amazing talent you have. These stories are nothing short of astonishing. You should write them down." John held her hand for a second too long after she was already back on her feet, making Emma blush.

"I didn't come up with them. It wouldn't be right to take the glory from their real authors."

"We still love them. It is such a blessing to have you with us. I hope you never leave," Agnes said before kissing her brother goodnight on his cheek.

"Do not be selfish, Agnes. Emma will have to find a suitable husband, and with her charms and looks, I would not be surprised if even the famous Duke of Davenport himself proposed to her. Unless she fancied something a bit closer?" Lady Evergreen said, waving her hand fan and trying to look innocent.

"Mother...pleeeeeaaaaaaase!"

John seemed to be at his wit's end with the amused Lady Evergreen, who kissed her son goodbye and excused herself, dragging Agnes along with her.

John turned to Emma after his mother and sister were through the door. "I apologize. For all intents and purposes, I truly do not know how to make her stop. Any suggestions would be greatly appreciated. With all your talents, I am certain you might have a few ideas? At this point, I am open to *anything*." John seemed half-joking and half-desperate.

Emma laughed. "I'm afraid it's every mother's duty to embarrass her children. They take this obligation very seriously, as you know." Emma helped Tilly clean up the pillows that some of the children had been sitting on. By now, Tilly knew not to argue with Emma that this was no task for a lady, as Emma would help her anyway. Tilly put the last pillow back on a chair next to the door and threw John a look that said, *"Do not let that one go,"* before leaving as well.

"That makes perfect sense. What about your mother? Is she as annoying as mine?"

Emma froze in sadness. The thought of her poor mother made its way into her mind quite often. Was she looking for her? Had the police gotten involved? She must be on the brink of losing her mind. She wasn't the best mother, but she loved Emma nonetheless and had done what she could to protect her from that joke Emma refused to call a father.

"I do beg your pardon. I did not mean to upset you. Really, when it comes these matters, I'm a fish out of water." John took a step toward Emma, as if he wanted to comfort her but didn't know how without being inappropriate.

"It's all right. She doesn't know I'm here."

"I'm ever so sorry. We do not have to talk about it," John said, his voice low with sympathy.

Emma did prefer not to talk about her mother. It broke her heart every time she thought of her. John took another step closer to Emma, taking one of her hands in one of his own, which caught Emma by surprise.

"I wish I could take your pain away. I feel so helpless when I see you sad."

Emma looked up into his beautiful eyes, so full of love and compassion. Never in her life had she craved the touch of a man more. What if she were to take a step closer and just put her head against his chest? Would he mind? Think her improper?

"Nobody has ever been this nice to me. I will never be able to repay you. Not in a million years would I have ever even dreamt it possible to meet someone like you." Emma meant it. Besides her mother, nobody had ever cared for her the way the Evergreens did. John pulled her hand up to his chest. She could feel his heartbeat. Its rhythmic pulsing intoxicated her. Her own heart started to beat faster.

"It seems Agnes is quite successful at making you believe all those exaggerated nonsense stories. But if they are convincing you to stay, then I swear by all that is dear to me, they are nothing but the truth." He smiled, taking another step closer, placing himself right in front of her.

She could smell him—gosh, he smelt good. He was at least a head taller than she was, as if he were made for women to lean their heads against his chest to find the comfort they craved.

"You are a kind and good man. You will make a special lady the happiest woman on earth one day." This very sentence brought Emma back into reality, as if she was hit with a cold bucket of water. What was she doing? She tore herself away from the sweet, intoxicating warmth of John's body, stepping backward before their bodies could touch.

That was exactly what she was not here for! Playing with John's feelings! She was not the woman who would make him happy. She was the woman who would break his heart and abandon him overnight whenever her first chance to go back home presented itself.

John took a step closer again. "Emma…I wanted to talk to you about something."

She pulled her hand free from his grip. "I…I better go see if Ackley was able to talk to the police about the robbers." Out of all the excuses in the world to leave, Emma had chosen this one, almost as if she wanted to remind herself once more that she was just a fraud.

"Of course," John said in a perfect gentleman's tone, despite her claim being an obvious excuse.

Naturally, the police wouldn't have new information about the robbers because they weren't real. *Just like you, Emma*, she told herself, rushing out of the room.

John was sitting in the library, reading over the same tenant contract over and over again. It was late, and everybody was in their rooms. He had the usual fire burning in the library's enormous fireplace. He sat there every evening with his whiskey to go over work he had missed during the day. But right now, he was incapable of doing even the slightest bit of work. His thoughts were completely occupied with beautiful, kind Emma. All week, Emma had let his overbearing sister and mother dress her in Davenport's dresses like she was a doll. John had never been interested in fashion, especially not Davenport's, but he had to admit, he loved every single one of the countless times his mother and sister had presented Emma to him in another dress. *How can she be so beautiful?* he wondered every single time she stood before him.

John had signaled to Emma on several occasions that he would come to her rescue and stop the fashion party of horrors, but she always turned him down with a kind smile, saying she enjoyed seeing his mother and sister so happy. John knew how trying his mother and sister could be, but he loved them, and they had pure hearts. For Emma to be so kind to them meant a lot to him. Nobody else in society was.

He shook his head to free himself of Emma for a moment, just to fall right back into the memories of her rolling around in the grass, playing baseball with the children. Her dress always got covered in grass and practically ruined, but Emma never paid it any attention. Once, she tickled little

Timmy until he dropped the ball, then ran off with it, chased by a horde of screaming children. Like a fopdoodle, he would stand by the window or lean against a wall to watch her play this wild American sport or exciting card games with the children, simply unable to tear himself away.

John suddenly thought about the dreadful Davenport party tomorrow. If not for Emma and his mother and sister, he wouldn't go there even if his life depended on it. Of course, Emma had no clue, but Davenport was the reason for everything that his family had gone through all these years. Only three people on this planet knew what had happened between John and Davenport, and neither his mother nor sister were one of them, so how could he possibly be mad at them for chasing after the duke like children chasing after a colorful butterfly? He couldn't, so he just watched in silence when they invited him into his house, accepted his invitation as though it was the greatest honor of their lives, and marveled at his presence as if they had come from the Lord savior himself.

John rubbed his forehead in disbelief of all the things that were going on right now. Emma took his breath away — Christ, she had even gotten him to accept an invitation to a party thrown by the only person on this planet he couldn't stand. All she had to do was look at him with her green eyes, and he would do anything for that woman. For some peculiar reason, it felt as if he'd known her for a long time. He felt comfortable around her, craved her company, her touch.

John pushed the contract aside as though it had just defeated him in a round of chess. He took a long sip from his whiskey and folded his sleeves up to his elbows to look at the wound the drunken fool Milly had given him when John pulled him out of the gutters. It was red but not infected. He threw his head back and stared at the ceiling, thinking again about those eyes and pretty smile that always warmed his heart.

"You are a fool, John," he said to himself, thinking that the very thing he'd tried to avoid all his life had happened to him in a matter of days. He'd fallen in love. But what if she didn't return his feelings? Her eyes told him that she wanted him as much as he wanted her, but the way she had acted in the music room today implied otherwise. And what if she fell for the duke? He'd surely done everything he could to make it happen. That buffoon had danced in front of her with everything he had, like one of these brightly colored birds trying to attract a female for mating season. It was so unlike Davenport, who did nothing for anybody—ever—period. Was this directed at John, or did he really feel—whatever the duke was capable of feeling—for Emma?

The door squeaked and opened slowly. And there she was. Emma Washington.

"Oh, I am so sorry. I didn't mean to intrude." She turned around to leave, but John jumped up.

"No, please. You have not intruded at all."

"It was just, I couldn't sleep. And Lily told me that every fine house has a library, so I thought I might borrow a book."

John instantly took a few steps from the couch he had been sitting on to invite her to come in and take a seat. "You are at the right place for that. Come in and look around. Or take a seat and tell me what books you like to read, and I can tell you what books we have that might be a good fit for you. You see, I know this library better than it knows itself," John said proudly with a smile.

Emma sat down and scanned the library. "It's quite impressive. I mean, having so many books."

John sat down on the couch across from her. She was wearing a comfortable nightgown and had put her hair up in a lazy bun. He noticed that

119

she wasn't wearing a corset. She must have meant to quickly grab a book without being noticed by anybody. He could see the lines of her breasts through her gown, sending a heat wave through his inner thighs. John shifted his gaze to the more appropriate fireplace.

"So, how many of these books have you read?" Emma challenged him, the corners of her mouth ticking upward mischievously.

"All of them."

"All of them? But there must be thousands!"

"Eight thousand two hundred and forty-one, to be exact."

"That is incredible." Emma sounded genuinely impressed.

He folded his hands behind his head. "Ha! Before you admire me for something I am not worthy of, let me explain. I did not necessarily *read* them all. It would be more accurate to say I skimmed a lot of them."

She grinned. "That's still very impressive."

"Well, that is what happens when you have as many sleepless nights as I do."

Emma looked down at the carpet as if she wasn't sure to ask about those sleepless nights or not.

"You can ask if you want to, it is quite all right." Why did he want her to ask him about something he never spoke of with anyone? Even encourage her to ask? To this day, he told his closest friends and even his own mother that he didn't want to talk about his time in the army whenever the subject arose.

"Are nightmares the cause for all those sleepless nights?" This took John by surprise. Emma had said it so casually…as if it was totally acceptable to talk about it. She hadn't asked it in a way that seemed uncaring. It was more like she actually wanted to know what was troubling him.

"Yes. They are. From my time in the military. I am sure Agnes leaves those details out when she sings about those glorious medals of honor I brought home. But then, most people avoid taking the conversation about war further than the pretty parts. It does not make for nice dinner conversation to talk about the reality of war."

"Only the dead have seen the end of war," Emma said in an empathetic voice, moving John in a way nobody ever had before. If John didn't know better, he would think he was talking to a fellow soldier, someone who'd been there to see the horrors and truly understood how accurate Emma's summary of war was. If he hadn't understood his attraction to this woman earlier, without a doubt, he did now.

"I honestly would never have joined the military if I had not found myself in an unfortunate situation that required me to enlist. I had no part in causing this unfortunate circumstance, but the end result was the same." It mattered to John what Emma thought of him. For a moment, he was hesitant to share with her the reason that had forced him into war, what had happened between him and Davenport all those years ago, but then he decided not to. He didn't want to come off as a desperate rival who was trying to bad-talk his wealthier, more attractive opponent. Thank goodness Emma changed the topic, as if she knew that they were getting into territory that made John uncomfortable.

"What happened to your arm?"

"Oh, that? Let us just say, some people are easier to help than others." John walked over to a little wood table with different bottles of whiskey on it. "May I offer you a whiskey?"

"Yes, please."

"Ha! Why am I not surprised that you drink whiskey, Mrs. Emma Washington?" He laughed lightheartedly while he filled her a glass and refilled his as well.

"Is it inappropriate for ladies here in England to drink whiskey?"

He handed her the glass. "Unusual, not inappropriate. Most women prefer sweet champagne or wines."

"I have to confess, I prefer those over whiskey as well, but as we say where I'm from, a free drink is a free drink." Emma took a big sip.

He laughed. "I think I like Americans more and more by the minute. So, tell me, what kind of books do you like to read?"

He studied Emma, who took another big sip of her whiskey like it was water. She was obviously nervous about something. Was it the fact that they were alone together?

"Books about chemistry...and time tra...times. Books about different times. Or old rituals."

"That must be the most interesting combination of books I have ever heard."

John grinned and walked over to one of the many bookshelves next to the fireplace. "We have Dickens, Whitman, Herman Melville and Washington Irving. Oh, here we are. Books about chemistry would be here."

She joined him and moved her finger over a few expensive, leather-bound books. John couldn't help staring at her. The soft light of the fireplace made her face even more beautiful. It reflected a romantic, warm glimmer off her pretty lips.

His heart started pounding faster. By God, he wanted to kiss her right there and then. And before he even realized what he was doing, he grabbed her softly by her wrist and pulled her into his arms. She was so close, he could smell her breath, a mixture of whiskey and mint. There was no turning back now. Something else was controlling his body.

John tilted his head and leaned closer. What if he just gave her a soft kiss on the side of her neck? If he was gentle, maybe she wouldn't mind…

Emma felt John's lips on the side of her neck, running softly down to her collar bone, sending tingling shockwaves from her stomach into her hands and feet. She moaned in pleasure and threw her head back, signaling him how much she wanted him.

He kissed her neck again, moving upward toward her face until his lips finally found hers. He brushed his lips against hers so gently, they barely touched.

She was burning. On fire. Breathing heavily, she pressed her body tightly against his. She was losing her mind—she wanted this man more than any other man before.

She grabbed his hips with both hands, guiding him toward the hot area between her legs. He followed her lead and placed his erection where she craved it the most. In response, she moved her hips in small, slow motions, rubbing against him. John groaned loudly, as if it was more than he could take.

"Emma," he whispered into her ear.

He grabbed her by her upper thighs and lifted her buttocks onto the library shelf, spreading her legs so he could fit in between her thighs. She'd never felt so aroused in her life. She needed to have him, or she would die of lust.

John was at the brink of losing his mind, something that had never happened to him before. The way Emma was rubbing against him, he could barely control himself any longer. He wanted to pull her undergarments down and enter her right there on the bookshelf like a wild animal.

Her legs were now wrapped tightly around his hips, as if she would never let go of him again.

"We have to stop," John growled into her ear.

"Please don't," Emma moaned back, her beautiful green eyes looking into his, full of passion.

She rotated her hips in a rhythm that grew faster and faster. His whole body was burning. This was the most intense feeling he had ever felt. He wanted to beg her to never leave. To stay here with him, so he could make love to her, kiss her, be with her every day for eternity.

Emma sank her fingers into John's backside, pressing herself against him as hard as she could.

"John—" she gasped loudly in the most sensual voice he had ever heard. She threw her head back in pleasure and said his name aloud again. He stared at her beautiful face, wanted to tell her how much she meant to him, but suddenly, a door slammed in the hallway.

"Emma?" Lily's voice sounded so close, she must have been right outside the library door. John froze in shock. He felt Emma do the same beneath him. Her face looked just as panicked as he felt. In a matter of seconds, he came to himself again, realizing where he was and what they were doing.

At once, he pulled away from Emma, who jumped off the bookshelf and tried frantically to make herself look presentable. John did the same. The door opened, and Lily stepped in, looking first at Emma and then at John, then back at Emma. There was no doubt; Lily knew exactly what they'd been up to. She grasped for words for a moment.

"I…I was looking for you, and then the wind slammed the door. I see you tried to get a book from the library?" Lily asked, playing innocent. Of course, nobody was buying it, but they all played along.

Emma cleared her throat to get her voice back to normal. Her cheeks were still red, and she had that certain glow around her that women got after they had felt the gentle touch of a caring man.

"Erm, yes…chemistry. I couldn't sleep, and you know how much I love my chemistry."

"Yes…it was quite hard. The books, I mean…" John shook his head in disbelief. "It was very *difficult* for Emma to find a book she liked." John had never sounded more like a fool than in this very moment. He grabbed a book from the very same area he had had Emma pressed against not even a minute ago. He handed it to Emma without looking at it. "Here it is. Finally found it."

"Yes, that's the one. Thank you." She read the title aloud in an attempt to convince Lily. "'Mating Behaviours of Insects in the Amazons.'"

Jesus, why did he grab that one, out of 8,241 books!

Emma accepted it with a little hesitation. "Yes, t-that's the one. Very interesting. Thank you." She walked straight past Lily and out the door.

Lily followed her, but not without smirking at John again before closing the door behind them.

She knew. *She knows exactly what just happened*, he scolded himself. He noticed that a few books had fallen from the bookshelf and grabbed one of them, but instead of putting it back, he threw it angrily back on the floor.

What had he done? He brought Emma into this house for safety from the very thing he had just exposed her to. He had pushed himself onto her as if he hadn't the slightest bit of control over his own body. His whole life, he'd been able to control himself. For years, he had turned down woman after woman—rich, poor, beauties, and ugly ones alike. All of them. And now, this! All it took was the presence of Emma Washington, and he wasn't himself anymore. Tomorrow, he would have to beg for forgiveness. Fall on his unworthy knees and apologize, promise it would never happen again. Promise he would do whatever Emma asked of him, including marriage. It was the right thing to do after dishonoring her like that. John repeated the thought in his head once more. Marriage. There it was. The very notion that had caused feelings of anxiety in him for years suddenly had a pleasant ring to it. He desired to marry her, not just to save her reputation, but also because he couldn't imagine life without her anymore.

But would Emma even have him? She must now think him a gal-sneaker. A flirt. A man who did nothing else but run after a skirt as if his life depended on it. He had done a marvelous job increasing Davenport's chances of winning Emma over. Tomorrow, he would make it right. Yes, tomorrow he would explain to her that he was not the man she must think him to be and that he had had feelings for her from the moment he first saw her. He would tell her that he was no Casanova. And, by all that was mighty and just, that was the God's honest truth. Emma was the first woman he'd ever lost control with. The first woman he had ever actually wanted to be with. To be truthful, Emma was the very first woman in his life — ever.

Many years ago, he had kissed a woman, but that had been the extent of it. Not because he was interested in men or because he couldn't get a woman to marry him. He had simply put marriage out of the cards for good after the whole Davenport incident.

Well, congratulations, John, he scolded himself. *It looks like you just got yourself a new hand of cards. Play them well, my friend. Play them well.*

CHAPTER 8

Emma was having the hardest time getting Lily to leave her be. All night and morning, she tried to have the one conversation Emma simply didn't want to have. Not with her and not with John.

Of course, Lily wanted to talk about what had happened between John and Emma in the library. Not so much the physical part; for a woman like Lily, there wasn't the smallest curiosity left concerning the physical interactions between a man and a woman. No, what Lily wanted to talk about was as clear to Emma as her feelings for John.

Lily wanted Emma to marry him. Tomorrow, if that was an option. She wasn't mad at Lily for trying. It was apparent how much Lily loved it here. She had mentioned at least nine times how nice the servants were to her. She even had her own room with a bed, if she wanted. And fresh rolls with cheese and bacon for breakfast. For Lily, who had literally come from nothing, that was a lot. So why didn't Emma marry John? She asked herself that same question over and over again, as if she was hoping for a different answer if she just kept asking.

"Because he deserves a woman who will be his wife, not use his money and status to find a way to abandon him the first chance she gets."

Lily raised a few valid points though. John wasn't some innocent eighteen-year-old. He'd probably been with plenty of women before and knew what he wanted. So did Emma. She knew that she wanted him. She knew that she cared for him. Just thinking about his beautiful brown eyes and the way he had looked at her last night made her tingle all over again. She also knew that John was an honorable man with a loving heart, and that was hard to find in a man, no matter the century.

But that was the issue. How could she marry him and then break his heart and embarrass him in front of society by disappearing back to the twenty-first century? Nobody knew who she was, and they wouldn't have a clue where she had gone. To everybody else, it would look like she had run off and would make John and his caring family the laughingstock of London. But what if she never found a way home? Wouldn't she rather be married to a man she cared for than be stuck for the rest of her life in Victorian England with Davenport?

No, she *would* find a way home. And that meant that she would have to marry the duke. The fact that there was some sort of beef between him and John made her feel even less guilty for using Davenport. The brute must have done something terrible to John. The way John looked at him made that very clear. There was no way John would feel contempt for someone without a damn good reason. He just was not that kind of person.

With a heavy heart, and ready to have the most uncomfortable talk of her life, Emma decided to join the Evergreens for breakfast like she did every morning. She would talk to John afterward and get it over with. Tell him sorry for last night. If he offered her marriage, thinking he had dishonored her, she would refuse his offer of marriage and tell him she wasn't some ruined virgin but a competent widow with a bright future ahead. Yes, that sounded great.

Emma settled on a dark-blue day dress that had a beautiful tail in the back, the height of fashion in the 1880s. Lily had Alice, one of Agnes's maids, help her put Emma's hair up into a decorative bun. The duke had even included jewelry in his *little* care package, as he'd called it. Emma was afraid to ask anybody if the diamonds were real because they sure as hell looked real to her. There was no doubt that Davenport was wealthy beyond what Emma was able to grasp. The end result of putting the *little* care package together on Emma in full glory was nothing short of stunning. She looked like a true lady, like a duchess. To be honest, she felt she looked like a woman who could get the richest and most handsome man in all of England to marry her. This was confirmed by the hysterical Evergreen ladies and John's facial expression when Emma joined them in the breakfast room.

"Oh, goodness, I have never laid my eyes upon a prettier lady before! You will have countless suitors to pick from today—won't she, John?" Lady Evergreen shouted proudly, as if Emma were her own daughter.

Emma shot John a guilty look, but he responded emotionlessly, "Yes, indeed."

The talk that Emma had wanted to have after breakfast never happened. John had successfully managed to avoid her all morning. They exchanged polite statements, and John did a fantastic job of acting totally normal. On one hand, Emma was grateful for that, as awkward silence between the two of them could have raised red flags in front of the staff or his family. On the other hand, however, Emma was also somewhat shocked that John was acting as if nothing had ever happened.

What if he didn't care about their passionate encounter? Or Emma? Maybe Lily was right after all, and John was a good fellow but also well aware of what he was doing, just like any other man. Wouldn't that mean that Emma could re-think marriage to him? That said, if he would ever propose...but so far, it didn't look like it. Maybe Emma was wrong about him, and he was just another man chasing skirts. His behavior surely seemed to confirm that. Why else would he avoid her, pretending nothing was the matter? Her heart felt as if someone had just stabbed it with a sharp knife. *Isn't that what you wanted? Keep John out of your life? Stop acting like a heart-broken teenage girl*, she told herself. Nonetheless, it still hurt like a broken heart. And maybe it was.

Around noon, Emma and the Evergreens headed out to the gathering at Blackwell Castle. Like a perfect gentleman, John helped her into the carriage. Emma could have slapped herself for feeling her cheeks turn red the moment their hands touched. She had to get the duke to marry her as soon as possible. What had begun as a mission to protect kind John from hurt feelings had turned into a potential broken heart on Emma's end. This rollercoaster of emotions had to stop — now.

Blackwell Castle was only thirty-five minutes away, and the ride went by quickly with Lady Evergreen and Agnes babbling nonstop about the Duke of Davenport's riches. So — Emma had thought she was prepared for what was to come but, hell, was she wrong. When the carriage pulled up in front of Blackwell Castle, Emma involuntarily cussed out loud in awe.

"Are you freaking serious?" She had never, absolutely *never*, seen a castle like Blackwell Castle. The *little* gathering, as Davenport had described it, was in reality a huge party. Carriages lined up in front of the enormous stairs that led up to wide-open, golden double doors. The sun reflected off those golden doors, briefly blinding people as they walked up the stairs. This was ridiculous.

Lady Evergreen grabbed Emma under her arm and walked her up the stairs to step into an entrance hall that made the castle in the show *Downton Abby* look like Lily's room. Artful decorations in gold and precious stones decorated the walls and ceilings. Were those diamonds?

Lady Evergreen whispered into Emma's ear, "The Blackwells are the most established family in all of England. Their roots go back hundreds of years. Rumor has it that not a single king of England has not borrowed money from them."

Emma had had no clue. Lily had left that detail out when they were sitting on the floor in her dark, cold flat, planning the ultimate escape from the slums of London. Was she up for this task? For the first time, Emma started to really doubt herself.

"Mrs. Washington!" Davenport shouted over to her from a parlor filled with society's finest. "Let me help you."

He rushed over to take Emma's cloak and hand it to a servant.

"You look stunning!" William said, a bit flirty.

"Thanks to you," Emma flirted back.

The game was on. Emma was now fighting for more than her and Lily's survival and her chance of getting back home. She was fighting to flee from Evergreen, a former sanctuary that had now placed a big target on her heart. Emma took the duke's arm, and he led her through a golden parlor, past the whispers and icy stares of everybody in it. She and Davenport were the center of attention, something he was obviously used to. He stopped in front of two elegantly dressed women, who instantly analyzed Emma from head to toe. One was older but still beautiful, and the other was young and pretty. Both of them had black hair and icy blue eyes. Emma knew what was up.

"Now, you must be the famous Mrs. Washington my son is so taken with. I now see why. Very agreeable indeed, so to speak," the Duchess of Davenport said with a fake smile. No doubt, the duchess was a woman of the highest class in England. She must have been a remarkable beauty in her day, a trait she had handed down to both of her children.

"You certainly were not lying, William, when you said that Mrs. Washington is the most beautiful woman you have ever laid eyes upon," Davenport's sister said.

"Mrs. Washington, may I introduce my mother, and sister, Alvina."

"It's a pleasure meeting you both," Emma replied politely.

"One might almost think her a lady of society from looking at her," Alvina said, waving her fan in an arrogant gesture.

"Indeed, very un-American looking, so to speak," the duchess agreed with her daughter.

And there it was. Emma was not surprised at all about this not so subtle insult. Obviously, both ladies were used to getting their way, and right now, Emma was confident that their way did not include a marriage between Emma and Davenport. That was something Emma could actually understand and sympathize with. The duke's family was the most respected family of the country, and his mother would probably approve of nothing less than a princess for her son.

Unfortunately for the duchess, Emma had just time-traveled after getting hit by a car, and on top of that, she had the responsibility of saving a kind-hearted prostitute by finding a way back to the future for both of them. In short, she was in battle mode, and she was here to win this fight or die trying. Besides, thanks to his status, Davenport's reputation would recover in no time, should

Emma ever make it back home. And William Blackwell surely wouldn't be heartbroken for long. It might even teach him the lesson of what it feels like to suffer from a broken heart—a misery plenty of women had surely endured thanks to him.

No, Emma's sympathies did not go as far as calling it off to save privileged Duchess of Davenport's feelings. The law had to be laid out right here and now, in front of everybody. Emma had to prove herself and also test out the waters to see how the duke would respond to her challenging his mother and sister.

"Thank you. One might almost think both of you American from your ability to shoot. Verbally, at least," Emma said, copying Alvina's arrogant hand fan movements.

She glanced at Davenport, who stared at her in a mix of admiration and amusement. She had bet everything on this moment, and she'd played her cards well. Davenport was exactly who she had thought he would be. He felt challenged; she could see the need to tame her, possess her, in his eyes.

"What a suiting comment for the opening of our hunting season party," the duke said with a big smile, facing the crowd that had witnessed the exchange between Emma and the duke's sister and mother.

"Let us show you around before the concert," he said, leading Emma out of the golden parlor and on to a personal, private tour of the Blackwell estate. Emma tried to scout John in the crowd, but he was nowhere to be seen.

The tour of Blackwell Castle was surprisingly enjoyable. Not because it might all be hers soon or because Davenport was such a pleasure to be around, but because of its west wing. The west wing used to belong to the duke's father, who'd passed a few years ago. Apparently, the former duke had had a deep and passionate love for archeology and had formed a collection of rare and antique artifacts from all over the world. Emma couldn't think of a better place to start her research on how she had come to be here. Was this a sign that she was on the right path? Davenport was not precisely what she would go for if she had a choice, but beggars couldn't be choosers.

The tour led Emma by the gardens, past the target-shooting area set up to open the hunting season and ended in the music parlor. People were already seated in front of a grand piano that was accompanied by a beautiful blonde woman.

With a slim figure and sharp, pretty features, she looked the absolute perfect lady of society.

"Here." The duke handed Emma a glass of champagne.

She tried to find the Evergreens, which wasn't hard, thanks to Lady Evergreen's love for colorful dresses. Emma's heart dropped when she noticed that John wasn't with them. Where the hell was he? She hadn't seen him all day, despite the Blackwell tour making plenty of stops to engage in small talk with people spread all over the property.

Emma saw Agnes and Lady Evergreen sitting down next to the duke's sister and mother, who did not seem to approve of this at all. She couldn't hear what words were being exchanged between them, but whatever they were, it made Agnes and Lady Evergreen get up and smile, clearly embarrassed, before sitting down somewhere else. People who had witnessed the whole scene laughed and giggled openly. Emma felt anger. No, *rage*. How dare those arrogant Blackwells treat the Evergreens like this!

Luckily, the concert started before Emma could walk over and call the duchess out on her impossible behavior. That would not have gone well for Emma, but she would have done it anyway.

The blonde woman had a beautiful voice. She sounded like an angel, singing Italian and German arias. People stood up after she finished, applauding in amazement. She gave elegant curtsies and bows before leaving the stage. Suddenly, the blonde beauty's gaze targeted Emma and Davenport, and she walked straight toward them.

"William, what a delight to see you. We were so pleased to receive your invitation. It has been so long," she said in a soft, polite tone.

William didn't say a word back to her.

Emma's fine and highly accurate *drama* alarm bells went off, big time. Something was going on here.

"And this must be the famous Mrs. Washington, all the way from America?" the lady asked to break the awkward silence the duke had created.

"I'm afraid so," Emma said carefully, not sure what was going on here.

"It would be a pleasure to thank your husband for joining us today. Is he not here with you, Elise?" Davenport said in a condescending way that almost sounded like a warning.

Elise seemed to understand his warning perfectly well. "Unfortunately, he is not up to dick."

"Unfortunate indeed. Well, next time, then. Will you excuse us?" Davenport said, grabbing Emma's arm, but Elise wasn't finished yet.

"Of course, but I was hoping to get a taste of Mrs. Washington's accomplishments," Elise roared over the din of chatter.

The room grew quieter, and some people started to gather around Emma.

"Do they not teach a lady how to entertain in America?" Elise shouted at Emma, making sure that now every soul in the room made Emma the focus of their attention. Elise's grin confirmed that this was exactly her intention. The room dove into pin-drop silence.

Why did Elise want to embarrass Emma? What was it between her and Davenport that made her so jealous?

"Piano, singing, dancing...surely there must be something American women are good at?"

People started to laugh.

"I could not think of a more exciting way to pass time than to learn about the accomplishments of a lady from so far away, so to speak," the duchess agreed loudly as she and her snobby daughter Alvina stepped a little bit closer. They seemed to be truly enjoying Elise's attack on Emma, as if it were payback for losing to her earlier.

What was Emma supposed to do? She was a typical twenty-first-century woman. What average modern woman could play the piano or dance some old Victorian ballet?

"I am afraid I am not a very good singer or pianist," Emma said nervously. Was she about to be defeated by a most likely burnt-out former flame of the Duke of Davenport? Did everything end right here and now in embarrassment? People started to whisper, trying to hide their laughs behind their hand fans.

"Well, what are you American women good at? Shooting pistols wildly into the air like cowboys?" Elise rejoiced in the loud, uncontrolled laughter that now spread from person to person like wildfire.

Emma looked around at the crowd and finally found long-lost John standing next to the balcony door. He wasn't laughing nor whispering like the others; he was looking in disgust at the people around him. John locked onto Emma's gaze, looking at her as if he was ready to take her away from it all. Back home. Emma felt her wits come back to her, and she said smoothly, "Not wildly."

The room grew quiet.

"Excuse me?" Elise drew her brows together in confusion.

"I said, not wildly. If you want to learn about an American lady's accomplishments, I am afraid you will have to follow me." Elise looked just as bewildered as everybody else. Emma broke free from Davenport's grip around her arm and walked out onto the balcony. People chased after her like chickens following a trail of corn. Emma made her way down the enormous stairs that led to the target-shooting area set up in the gardens.

Davenport had walked her past this area earlier, explaining that the season always started with a shooting competition. The winner would get the honor of choosing a horse for the hunt, which would usually be the impressive beast, Thunder.

People were chattering uncontrollably when Emma walked over to a table that had different pistols and rifles lined up. Some of the rifles looked similar to what her dad had used for hunting—and teaching her how to shoot.

Emma's father had never done anything fun with her. No birthday parties, no bike rides, no fun teatime with dolls. But the one thing his delusional mind had taught her was how to shoot. Not because he wanted to share his interests with her. No...Emma's crazy father was a huge conspiracy theorist. He prepared for the end of the world as if it could happen at any moment. She couldn't be a burden during the zombie apocalypse, so he had taught her how to shoot— extremely well. Like her life would depend on it someday. Funny enough, it kinda did now.

Emma chose a rifle that looked similar to the Winchester her father had. She'd shot her very first target with it when she was barely seven years old. She walked up to the line on the grass that indicated where to shoot from. There were five round targets that definitely classified as middle- to long-range. Probably about a thousand feet away. She positioned the rifle against her shoulder, leaning her face over it just enough to get a clear view of the five targets through the sight ring that was mounted at the end of the barrel.

Emma then turned around again and surveyed the crowd, looking for the very thing that would help her determine the direction and strength of the wind. She didn't have to look very long. Emma walked up to an older gentleman and grabbed his burning cigar out of his mouth. He stared curiously at Emma, who walked back to position herself behind the line on the ground again. She held the cigar up against the wind for a few seconds. That was all the information she needed.

"Moderate wind conditions from the west. Targets about a thousand feet away," Emma said confidently.

She dropped the cigar onto the grass, tensed her muscles to hold the rifle in its place, and squeezed the trigger. Not once, not twice—she emptied all five rounds. The noise of the shots made some ladies squeak in fear like little piglets. She allowed no breaks between shots. She sighed, shifted, and squeezed, again and again. After the final bullet left the barrel, Emma analyzed the end result. All five targets were hit dead center, making it five perfect shots. She took a moment of silence to thank her crazy father for his totally nuts doomsday preparations and almost laughed out loud, thinking that it had saved her butt, not in an apocalyptic future, but in Victorian England—which was even crazier.

The crowd's silence broke into loud cheers and ecstatic clapping.

People were shouting, "Bravo!"

"Outstanding!"

"Incredible!"

Emma picked the cigar back up from the ground and returned it to the older man, who was clapping frantically along with everyone else. She then turned to Elise, who was standing next to the Blackwell ladies. All three of them looked like little kids who had just been sent to their rooms.

"As I said—Elise, was it? Not wildly." Emma dramatized her American accent a bit with pride.

She promptly turned on her heel from the trio of snakes and joined Lady Evergreen and Agnes, offering each of them her arms. Both accepted in excitement, holding their heads up high. Emma glanced at the duke. He wasn't clapping, but his face was a mixture of pure pride and satisfaction. He gave Emma a silent well-done head nod.

Where was John? It took Emma a bit to find him standing far off in the crowd, at the top of the stairs to the balcony. He wasn't smiling or clapping. Emma's heart flinched. Why not? Wasn't he proud of her? At least entertained? Emma looked back at him several times before the Duke of Davenport managed to drag her back inside, leaving behind a crowd of ladies and gentlemen who started shooting at the targets in an attempt to beat Emma's record.

Davenport walked Emma to the portrait gallery of Blackwell Castle. It was enormous. She wondered why he hadn't taken her here earlier when they toured the estate. He stopped in front of a massive portrait of a knight in black armor. It must have been from medieval times, according to the primitive painting techniques used in it.

"This is the very first Blackwell," he said, full of pride. He took a few steps closer to the painting, which must have been double his size. "Story has it that he killed the dragon that stole the future Queen of England from her king on their wedding night. The king was so grateful to have her returned safely that he swore to make the Blackwells the richest family in the country. Richer than himself."

Emma took a few steps closer to examine the painting in more detail. The story was actually quite fascinating. "It seems like the Blackwells make it a habit of saving women in need," Emma joked.

Davenport stayed serious. "People in this family have a duty, Emma," he said, calling her by her first name for the first time.

So, now we're on a first-name basis. That's good progress, she thought. William took a step closer and took her hand. Emma felt absolutely nothing.

"The duty to understand that we are better and more important than everybody else on this planet. People need to know who we are; people need to know who to bow to."

Wait…what? Dear God, did he really just say that? Emma almost stumbled backward in shock at the amount of arrogance she had just witnessed. If he would have spoken of honor, even looking the part…but to say that they were better than everybody else repulsed her. This was precisely the sort of thinking that led to hatred and war — closed minds lacking the ability to feel for others. And in front of her stood the very prototype of ignorance and entitlement.

Emma thought about all the times she'd gone through trash cans with her mother looking for food. All the times she had to wear shoes with holes in them to school, getting laughed at by her classmates. The freedom and relief she had felt when she received her first paycheck as a pharmacy assistant.

How could the duke be so far away from her reality...anybody's reality? Did he not know how many people were starving in the streets of London at this very moment? If she had ever had even the slightest bit of guilt for marrying Davenport just to leave him high and dry, that feeling was gone. She couldn't wait to teach this family a lesson, make them the center of a scandal. Emma almost smiled thinking about the gossip that would follow her disappearance into thin air. That would bring them down from their high horses, even if just for a little while. Let them know what it felt like to walk down here, amongst real people. People like Lily, who felt nothing but shame and pain day in and day out.

Emma took a deep breath, but instead of sealing the deal right there in front of an ugly painting, she said something that surprised her as well.

"Is Elise the reason why you and Evergreen don't get along?"

William took a step back, staring at her in astonishment before he started to smile.

"You are just too smart for your own good, aren't you? This is the reason why I brought you here. I could have brought many women here, including Elise. But I was waiting—waiting for a woman like you, Emma. A woman who is not only superior in looks but also in her will and intelligence. A true Blackwell."

Emma stayed quiet, signaling to William that he hadn't answered her question yet. He got the hint.

"Yes. She is. It happened many years ago. It was quite an annoyance, to be honest with you. Back then, John and I were young men, barely leaving childhood behind us. We were sort of friends, if you want to call it that. Against my advice, John was secretly engaged to Elise. I tried to warn him, tell him that she was not worth his while, but John is a very stubborn man. Unfortunately, I was right about Elise all along, and she decided to fall in love with me. Who would not want to be a Blackwell and my duchess? So, it was quite understandable."

Emma wanted to roll her eyes but was able to control herself. William continued.

"She called off her engagement to John before he could announce it. She was a fool if she even thought for a second that I would marry her. I sent her away. Told her to go back to John, that I would never marry her. What happened after that between the two of them, I am not sure. All I know is that Elise started to spread rumors about the Evergreens that almost ruined the family. John went off to war and came back a hero to save his family's honor. We have not spoken ever since. Until you came along."

That all sounded like something Thunder would drop from his behind to Emma, but what was she supposed to do? Call him out? Upset him so he would take back the offer of marriage that was about to come? William pulled Emma closer toward him before she could say anything. He was about to kiss her. Things were going as planned. So why was she carrying an immense feeling of guilt? Like she was cheating on John? She owed him nothing! Last night, they'd made out passionately, and today he'd ignored her as if nothing had ever happened.

Emma tried to tell herself to seal the deal with Davenport. Right here, right now. *Forget John. This is what you wanted, what you need to go home.* Emma tried to prepare herself for the kiss, but right before their lips touched, her body took over her mind, and she pulled away.

"I...I...I'm sorry. My head is spinning." Emma could have slapped herself. What was she doing? William's face went from passion to disappointment in the space of a heartbeat.

"Of course. You need to rest. I shall inform the Evergreens to take you back home," he said, kissing her hand like a gentleman. "I shall call on you tomorrow," William said, clearly unsatisfied with Emma's reaction to his attempted kiss.

He wasn't the only one frustrated by all of this. Emma was upset with herself. Her and Lily's future depended on this. Emma had pulled off what many would have considered impossible, and now she was risking it all—for what?

The answer was written all over her heart. John Evergreen.

CHAPTER 9

John had rarely felt more disheartened. All day, he had wanted to talk to Emma but didn't know how to. No, that wasn't quite the truth. All day, he had been avoiding Emma because he was afraid she would answer his marriage proposal with a "no." How could he blame her, after what had happened last night? And if that wasn't enough, Davenport's annual hunting celebration was pure hell.

Davenport was all over Emma, who seemed to be quite taken with him. Of course, the duke didn't miss a single chance to grin in John's face about the whole thing, as if he was saying, "I shall take her from you as well."

And for the grand finale of this intolerable day, Elise was at the bloody party too. He would have thought that after all the drama she caused ten years ago, she would have sat quietly in a corner hoping nobody would notice her. But that couldn't have been further from the truth. Not only did Elise try to challenge Emma publicly, but she also spent the remainder of the day stalking John to engage him in conversation. It was like playing hide and seek with the devil.

John couldn't remember another time he had suffered like this. Not even his time in the army had strained him emotionally as much as this afternoon. He couldn't stand still, as every moment meant anxiety-provoking thoughts running through his head.

The ride home in the carriage also proved unbearable. Emma sat right next to him, and he could feel the warmth of her leg against his, which automatically took him back to last night. The thought of that very same leg wrapped around his hips had him so aroused he was using every bit of willpower he had left to not get hard in the carriage. John would have to talk to Emma as soon as they got back. It was a lose-lose situation, so why not just get it over with?

The carriage arrived late, but still early for having come from a party at the Duke of Davenport's castle. Usually, those lasted until the early morning hours, as everybody wanted to make it last for as long as possible. Everybody but John.

He wanted to help Emma out of the carriage, but she stepped out so fast, he couldn't even offer her his hand.

"I'm tired. Please, excuse me," she said quickly before walking straight up the stairs to her room.

Great. How would he talk to her now? Lily was staying with Emma in her room, so it would be highly inappropriate to knock at her door late at night. But then, her maid already knew what was going on, so after going back and forth, John decided to take that risk. He would wait until his mother and sister went to bed and then knock at Emma's door to apologize...and somehow throw a marriage proposal in as well.

All his life, he'd tried to avoid marriage, but whenever he thought of Emma, he wanted nothing more than hold to her in his arms, to fall asleep next to her for the rest of his life.

It took his mother and sister longer than usual to go to bed. Their chatter about the Blackwell party hadn't died down, even long past their usual bedtime. John became extremely irritable with them and had to remove himself from the music room to avoid getting into it with his sister Agnes, who couldn't stop her babbling about the glorious William Blackwell. He had to remind himself over and over again that they didn't know about the whole Elise drama, so becoming heated with them was not appropriate.

It must have been around ten when the house finally settled down, and John was able to carefully knock at Emma's door.

"Emma," he whispered.

No answer. He knocked again.

"Emma, are you awake?" He waited for a few seconds. Nothing. She must have been asleep. He could have kicked himself for not talking to her earlier.

You're able to charge into battle with an empty rifle and a dull knife, but you're not capable of talking to the woman you want to marry? Have you turned into a coward?

"Well done, John...well done," he said to himself, walking to his room to prepare for a night full of torment.

Emma was in her nightgown and brushing her hair when she heard John knock on her door. She immediately signaled Lily not to open it. He knocked again, but Emma didn't move an inch.

He didn't knock a third time, but Emma and Lily still waited a bit longer, until they were sure he was gone, before Lily broke the silence.

"Emma, just go to him. Don't be poked up. You must talk to him and make things right."

"Poked up?" Emma asked.

"Embarrassed," explained Lily.

That was what Emma wanted as well, but what exactly was *right*? All day he'd ignored her and pretended like everything was blue skies and roses. Of course she was embarrassed.

"And then what?" Emma asked, putting the hairbrush down.

"And then you will marry Davenport and find a way home. For both of us, I hope."

Emma didn't respond to that.

"Or you will accept Evergreen's proposal and spend as much time as possible with the man you love before going home," Lily said, sitting down next to Emma on her bed.

"Love? That is ridiculous! And I don't even think he will propose!" Emma acted outraged, but Lily put a hand on her shoulder.

"Is it? You believe me when I tell you that love matters are my profession, do you not?"

Emma nodded her head.

"Well, then let me tell you that this man is just as much in love with you as you are with him. To be quite frank, I have never seen two people so obsessed with one another. It is like out of a Jane Austen novel."

"Wait...you know Jane Austen?" Emma asked, surprised.

"Of course. There isn't a single woman in town who doesn't dream of a romance like that."

"Then you should know that those romances aren't real," Emma said with a heavy heart.

"That's what I thought until I got to witness Mrs. Emma Washington and John Evergreen meet one another."

Emma quietly bit her lip.

"You know, he is not some little boy who can't make his own decisions. And if you're so worried about hurting his feelings, why don't you tell him the truth and let him choose for himself?"

"Tell him who I am? Where I came from?"

"Why not? You could show him the music box to prove that you are telling the truth. I could testify on your behalf."

Emma thought about it for a second. If this was a Jane Austen novel, she would just tell John that she was from the twenty-first century and had time-traveled here after getting hit by a car—which she would also have to explain. Then she would tell him how she planned to marry an arse with money so she could find a way back home into the future. Yes, in a romance novel, John would believe her and tell her that he wanted to be with her no matter what, even if it was only for a short while—or however long it took her to get back home.

But this wasn't some romance novel. Emma had woken up in the slums of London, facing prostitution. She knew she wasn't cut out for being a Victorian-era prostitute. God, she wouldn't have even made it until Christmas. Her twenty-first-century immune system was used to extremely high hygienic standards and antibiotics, so she would most likely have caught some infection that the people living in the slums of London were immune to and died miserably before the year was over. No, this wasn't a romance novel. But then, this was also not the world she used to know. She'd time-traveled after getting hit by a car, for heaven's sake. Anything was possible. Lily was right. She needed to talk to John and either tell him the truth or tell him that she would marry William Blackwell. No more games.

Emma made her way to John's room, walking as if the floor was made of eggshells. She didn't want to wake anybody, as it wasn't exactly ladylike to be seen at a man's room at night. But just when she was about to knock quietly on his door, she saw a light from a candle come around the corner down the hallway. Without thinking, she swung John's door open and closed it quickly behind herself, listening with her ear against the door to see if whoever was out there had seen her.

"Emma?" John asked, surprised. She turned around to apologize for her rude entry but froze before getting a word out. John was only partially dressed, wearing nothing but trousers. He was sitting in a chair in front of the fireplace. The warm, flickering light of the fire was dim but still bright enough to expose his whole upper body — covered in scars.

Emma took a few steps closer. It looked terrible. Not because it made him hideous or disfigured his muscular abdomen, no. It was more that Emma couldn't imagine the pain of what would cause such deep, long scars. There were too many to count. They ran all the way from his neck into his trousers.

"John, I had no idea…"

It seemed to take John a moment to understand what she was referring to. "Oh, that. It looks a lot worse than it is. It doesn't hurt at all. At least, not anymore. Really."

Emma walked over to him, close enough to be in his reach.

"What happened?" She felt a painful lump in her throat just thinking about the pain he must have endured.

"It happened on a mission in the Far East. Our troops were sent to take a town controlled by the rebels. If you want to call them that, but to be honest, looking back, they were just people trying to defend their families. Most of us knew it was a trap and that we would be horribly outnumbered.

We tried to convince our general to wait for reinforcements, but he was a stubborn old man with more pride than brains. He did not listen and led hundreds of young men to their deaths for some made-up glory. I was one of the few lucky ones. A barrel of black powder exploded right next to me when we attacked, and when I woke up, I was in an army hospital with a letter on my nightstand rewarding me with a medal for bravery. They should have given it for foolishness because that's all the mission was."

Emma looked at John in admiration. Not because he was a war hero, but because he carried those scars with such modesty. Suddenly, she saw a flicker of shame in his eyes. He stood up to reach for his shirt, which was hanging from the chair he had been sitting on. Emma stopped him, grabbing his arm before he could get to it.

"Don't..." she said softly. She wanted to comfort him, prove to him that she cared for him with or without the scars. And before Emma could tell herself to be reasonable, she leaned her head forward and kissed the scar on his neck. John was so shocked at Emma's tender kiss, his entire body froze beneath her lips. She gently moved her lips down toward his chest. He let out a moan.

"Emma...you do not have to —"

She pushed him back into his chair, kneeling in front of him between his legs.

"But I want to."

As though in a trance, she continued kissing his chest, moving her mouth passionately over his soft, scarred skin. John growled from deep within his chest, which turned Emma on even more. Her whole body was on fire. The sheer thought of making love to him sent little waves of excitement through her. She gently kissed her way down his muscular abdomen and back up to his neck, carefully opening the first button of his trousers. John grabbed her hand to stop her.

"What are you doing?" he moaned in a hoarse voice that begged for more.

She shook his hand off and continued to open his trousers, button by button.

"I want you," she whispered as she brushed her lips onto his.

This was more than John could handle. If he'd ever had common sense or reason, it was gone.

He gently pushed himself up and maneuvered her onto her back on the floor. Kissing her, he swept his tongue deep into her mouth, his hand lifting her nightgown. She eagerly helped him and wiggled underneath him in anticipation. John pulled her undergarments down and positioned his hips between her legs. Putting his weight onto his left elbow to avoid crushing her beneath him, he gently tilted her face toward his so he could look her in the eyes when he finally entered her.

Her beautiful green eyes locked in on his. She took a sharp breath in, throwing her head back a little.

He was truly amazed. How could she be so beautiful? How did he get so lucky to have met her? He slowly started to move inside her, whispering words of love in her ear. Emma's breath became louder and heavier, sending John's whole body into a tingle that felt as if butterflies were trapped inside him. She started to rotate her hips faster and faster, forcing John to adjust his rhythm according to her lead.

"Please don't stop," Emma murmured passionately.

John felt a wave of heat rise from his abdomen, spreading quickly through his whole body.

"I love you," he moaned against Emma's lips as he pushed over the edge.

Emma closed her eyes. It was the most intense feeling she had ever felt. Hearing John say those words against her lips made her climax with him. It was an overwhelming release of pleasure. A firework of joy and excitement.

She twitched underneath him, shaking uncontrollably for a few seconds. Then she looked up at him. He started kissing her again. She kissed him back, slowly releasing him from the firm grip of her legs.

He rolled next to her onto his side, maintaining their connection, his lips on hers. He was so gentle with her. Every touch was a statement of how much he cared for her.

John grinned. "This is not how I pictured my apology to you when I went over it a million times in my head."

His words tore her out of her dreamy world of love, and Emma remembered why she had come to his room in the first place. To talk to him, not to sleep with him. What had she done?

She pulled her nightgown down and sat up. John must have realized that there would be no holding each other until the morning, as he sat up as well, pulling his trousers back up.

Emma was close to tears. She had come to talk to him, to maybe even tell him the truth, but instead of making sense of things, she'd lost control again. *Don't you understand what is at stake here?*

"I'm so stupid," she said out loud, throwing her head into her hands. In a heartbeat, John was beside her. He put an arm around her and squeezed gently.

"You? For heaven's sake, Emma. The foolish one is obviously me. I brought you into my house to protect you, and then this happens? I barely recognize myself anymore…"

He seemed frustrated with himself, but she knew he shouldn't blame himself at all. Poor John had no clue that Emma was a sexually confident woman from the twenty-first century.

"It's not your fault, John. I'm a grown woman. I knew exactly what was going on. So please, don't feel like you have to apologize."

"You are quite right. I have to do a lot more than apologize to you. I should have asked you earlier, but I did not know how to. I was afraid you would say no to my offer of…"

Emma jumped up. "No...Please. Please don't offer me marriage. Not like this. You don't even know who I am. I won't trap you in a loveless marriage and then..." *Then what, Emma? Then leave him to return to the 21st century?* She couldn't finish that sentence. She simply didn't know how to.

John stood up as well and walked up to her. "Emma, I know this is not ideal. I cannot tell you how sorry I am that things went down this path. Normally, the man asks for the hand of a lady before the wedding night happens, but what's done is done. And the marriage would not be as loveless as you think, at least not on my end. I would not be a bad husband to you. I promise you that."

She remembered what he'd said to her just a few moments ago when they were united in passion.

John leaned forward and kissed her softly, and Emma felt that tingle in her stomach again. She opened her eyes slightly to look at his beautiful face. It would be nothing less than a dream to be married to a man like John. Maybe Lily was right. Maybe it wasn't so outrageous after all, to marry him. Emma would just have to tell him the truth.

"It wouldn't be loveless on my end either," she said in a tone that implied a *but*.

"Then what is it?"

Emma stayed quiet. John suddenly smiled at her with a big grin, as if he'd figured it out.

"If you have concerns that I am a gal-sneaker, let me tell you, it is quite the opposite. I have never been with a woman before, Emma."

Emma took a step backward. "You've never been with a woman before?"

"No."

"So…so this was your…"

"Very first time…yes. I hope it was enjoyable, or at least not terrible." He chuckled, and Emma turned away from him.

She started to grasp what she had done to him. John had just told her that he loved her, wanted to marry her. He had given her everything he had to offer, even what he had never given another woman before, and what had she given him in return? Lies, lies, lies. His heart would be broken no matter what.

She felt like a piece of shit. She had to come clean, now.

John watched her the entire time, trying to figure out what was on her mind. Suddenly, he walked up to the fireplace as if he had suddenly found the answer to the problem. He stared into the flames as though they would give him strength.

"Well, I did kiss a woman before."

Emma walked up to him. "Elise?"

"Ah...of course. Davenport told you, I assume?"

Emma confirmed with a nod.

"Well, I am sure he failed to mention that he seduced Elise in the back of a carriage when she was barely sixteen. Just a child. In all fairness, we were all children back then."

"I'm so sorry," Emma said empathetically.

"No need. I did not love her. My father and Elise's mother arranged a marriage between the two of us. To unite our estates. I was barely eighteen and agreed to it to make my father happy. He was a terrible man, and upsetting him would have made life hell for my mother and sister. He didn't care for treating women well."

Emma knew all too well what he was talking about. "So why did Davenport and Elise never get married? Did he straight out refuse to?"

"This is the part where things got ugly. If he had done the right thing and married her, things would have been different. Hell, my father might even still be alive. But no, not Davenport. Elise called a meeting with Davenport and me. I guess she wanted to come clean, thinking the duke would marry her. But the moment she told me about their love, Davenport started to laugh. He told her that she would never be the Duchess of Davenport and that she should crawl back to me. He said she would make an excellent Lady Evergreen, virgin or not. I would have fought Davenport right then and there, but Elise took off in a frantic state, so I went after her to make sure she would be all right.

The foolish part is, I would still have married her. I did not love her, but honestly, I never thought it fair for men to sleep around but deny women the same right before marriage, so I really did not care. To me, marriage was a business agreement.

But Elise turned out to be just as unreasonable as Davenport. She was determined to make him marry her. That is when these terrible rumors and lies about my family started. Horrible in nature. We soon discovered—they had come from Elise. To this day, I am struggling to understand why she did it. Maybe to focus her hatred on someone else, or maybe to ruin my family to force her mother to break off the engagement. Whatever it was, my father died of a heart attack shortly after, and my mother and sister were treated like outcasts and fell into deep depressions."

Emma kinda knew where this story was heading. Things were coming together like puzzle pieces now. "So, you joined the military to restore your family's honor?"

John nodded. "It was the only way. Nobody dares to disrespect war heroes. After my enlistment, the rumors stopped, and my family started to get invitations again. Elise had long disappeared, but rumor had it she married an Italian banker. And Davenport ...I had seen so much horror in battle. I decided to let go of my hatred for the duke and not challenge him to a duel. Besides, nobody knew about what had happened between us anyway. The engagement was never made public, and Elise disappeared to Italy for a few years after all of this, so society and my family thought she ran off with an Italian or something. So why open old wounds and drag my family though a scandal again?"

Emma threw her arms around John's neck and kissed him. She wanted nothing more than to comfort him. How could the world be so cruel to such a noble and kind man? He kissed her back as though it would help make all the bad memories disappear again. And had he stopped with his story right then and there, all would have been well. Emma would have told him the truth about herself and agreed to a marriage, but before she could even begin, John continued.

"And that is why I never married or let a woman near me again. Not because I was heartbroken, but I could not bear putting my family through something like that a second time. My father dead, my mother and sister outcasts, me trapped in the hell of war...and what for? All because a woman lied to me and then disappeared."

His words cut her like a sharp knife. Emma couldn't believe what he had just said. She tore herself away from John, almost losing her footing.

"What's wrong?" He tried to grab her hand, but Emma took another step back.

She was exactly like Elise. Different details, but the same ending. Nothing more, nothing less. Emma felt a burning sensation in her throat she knew would lead to tears. She turned around before John could see her like this.

"I'm sorry, John. I can't marry you!" Emma cried, storming out of his room. John tried to go after her, but Emma ran back to her room and locked her door.

"Emma!" John banged his fist against her door. "Emma, open the door and talk to me! Please!"

Emma did no such thing. Tears were running down her face. She threw herself onto the bed and sobbed into the pillows. How could she have thought for even a second that she and John could work out? She had ruined everything.

Maybe it would be best to just go back to London with Lily and do whatever work would pay for a room and a piece of old bread. At least then she would live life as it is, not waste her time on dreams and fantasies. She wanted to go back home. *Now.* Leave everything behind. John, William, Victorian London…all of it. Emma didn't notice when John stopped begging her to let him in, nor how long it took to cry herself to sleep. All she could hear were her father's words in her head, over and over again:

You are a Washington, so you will live in misery, just like the rest of us.

CHAPTER 10

"Emma…" Lily whispered. "Emma, wake up. Hurry."

E mma opened her swollen eyes. She must have cried for hours. It was still dark inside her room.

"We have to go, now," she heard Skip whisper.

Skip? What the heck was he doing here? Emma sat up abruptly.

"Skip? What are you doing here?" Emma barely recognized his silhouette in the dark.

"We have to go. Now. I shall explain later."

She got out of bed and grabbed one of her day dresses. Which one, she couldn't tell in the dark. Skip grabbed her hand to stop her.

"There's no time for putting that on. Pack as much as yer can. Only things of value."

Emma looked over to Lily, who was already frantically putting Emma's things in a bag. Skip helped her throw the first bag out the open window into the dark, cold night. Emma grabbed her cell from underneath the chair, where she had hidden it when she first got there. Trying to be as quiet as possible, she then packed the jewelry box and as many clothes as she could. Emma filled a whole bag with Davenport's gifts before Skip grabbed her by her arm.

"Shhh. Don't move."

Emma and Lily froze in fear. Footsteps from the hallway. They stopped near her door. Emma held her breath. If the servants or the Evergreens saw her like this now, they would probably call the police, thinking she was a fraud. Which she was.

The footsteps continued on, away from Emma's door. Skip signaled her and Lily to get out the window, throwing the bag Emma had just packed over his shoulder. Lily was halfway out the window, stepping onto what looked like a ladder of sorts. Emma followed her quickly, climbing out the window and onto the ladder herself. She wasn't afraid of heights, and the fall wouldn't have been very far, so she descended in haste and without care.

Skip was right next to them in a matter of seconds. He grabbed three bags and took off through the gardens to disappear into the dark shadow of the nearby woods. Emma grabbed the bag that was left and followed him, trying to watch every step as much as possible. That was easier said than done. The moon was hiding behind the clouds, making certain parts of the escape route pitch black. Just as she thought her eyes had somewhat adapted to the dark, her left foot got caught in some sort of bush, and she fell flat onto her arms and knees. Hard. Skip stopped and signaled Lily, who was right behind her, to help her back up.

"Are you all right?" she whispered.

Emma didn't think anything was broken but felt the familiar burn of flesh wounds on her knees and arms. There was no time now for booboos. She got back on her feet. "Yes, I'm fine."

The three continued to make their way like thieves through the night after a robbery. It must have been a good ten minutes before Skip led them into an opening next to a road. Emma saw the familiar carriage with the two brown horses that were complicit in what was supposed to have made her duchess and lady of Blackwell Castle.

Skip threw the bags onto the carriage and lit the lanterns that were attached to its sides.

"He knows," Skip said, strapping down the bags on top of the carriage to secure them.

"Who? John?" Emma asked in shock.

"Not sure about that. But Davenport does, for sure."

"But that's impossible," Lily said in disbelief.

"Nothing is impossible, especially when it involves that stinking son of a dog, Flinch."

"Who is Flinch?"

Lily's face became more and more the color of a tomato. She clenched her fists in rage. "Ooooohhhh, I will kill him!" she yelled, picking up a rock from the ground and throwing it angrily into the woods. "He ruined everything, the useless piece of shit!" she yelled, throwing another rock.

Emma looked at Skip. "Who is Flinch, and how does he know the Duke of Davenport?"

"The meater who tried to rob yer. Apparently, when yer were passed out on the side of a road or somethin'. The duke had a reward put out by his private detective asking for information regardin' a robbery on an American lady."

Emma didn't even have to hear the rest of the story. She got the picture. Flinch must have come forward and run his mouth. Emma sat down on the ground near Lily, who was still cussing and throwing rocks into the woods. She couldn't believe it. So, this was how it would all end? Send her to the poorhouse? Or into prostitution?

"Skip, when did all of this happen?" Emma asked.

"I cannot say for sure, but last night some time. I 'eard it early this mornin' from a friend. Said that Flinch came ter money for providing info on an American lady ter a private detective. The drunk fool that he is, he was runnin' his mouth in the Black Swan about it."

Emma didn't know what that was.

"A tavern," Skip explained.

Lily stopped throwing rocks and stomped over to Skip and Emma. "I shall kill him! I mean it," Lily clenched her fists again. She had tears in her eyes, and Emma knew why. It was all over. They would both spend their lives in Victorian poverty.

But...then why did Emma feel so calm? Almost relieved?

"Yer might not get that pleasure," Skip placed his hand on Lily's shoulder, a sign of sympathy. "He has disappeared."

"What do you mean?" Lily asked, wiping her tears away.

"Nobody really knows. He has not been seen since last night at the Black Swan. If we are lucky, he has succumbed ter the depths of the Thames. A fitting endin', considerin' how many people he and his crooked hornswoggler friends have robbed and thrown in there."

"So now Davenport has everything he needs to ruin us...or send us to prison." Emma couldn't make sense of it. She had been so close—why did this have to happen to her and Lily? How did they get so unlucky?

"Pretty much. A man like the Duke of Davenport can do whatever he wants with yer now. With his status and influence, he could have you locked up in his wine cellar if it pleased him. Or send yer ter an insane asylum, which would be worse than death, if you ask me," Skip said, shaking his head.

Emma understood perfectly well what a man like Davenport was capable of. And now that Emma had hurt his pride, even played him for a fool, he surely would not be happy about it.

"But maybe he doesn't care?" Lily sounded desperate, as if she was willing to grasp any bit of hope before she would return to a life of poverty and ruin.

"If that is the case, he will not care in a few weeks either and both of yer can come out of hiding. But for now, it would be better to get out of here. Better safe than sorry."

Emma agreed. If, for some reason, Davenport didn't care about the whole robbery plot and still wanted to marry her, it would still be an option in a few weeks. If, however, he were to use the information to slowly destroy Emma, then it would be better to be gone before he found out about it.

"Skip is right, Lily." Emma put a hand on her other shoulder to help Skip comfort her.

Lily seemed to calm down, slowly coming to terms with the situation. Anger and desperation turned into sadness, and she took a deep breath in and out.

"We were so close, Emma. Ever so close."

"I know…I know."

"We better go," Skip interrupted, jumping onto the driver's bench.

Lily stepped into the carriage, followed by Emma, who looked back onto the dark road as if she might see John there—for the last time. She thought about how badly she must have hurt him with all of this. She wished that she would never have tried to marry William Blackwell. She should have just lived her life in poverty and misery like all the other poor women in Victorian England. Like a true Washington, as her father would have told her.

As the carriage took off into the dark night, Emma swore to herself right then and there that she would never see John or William ever again. She would leave John be so he could find the woman he deserved. And William…no, she wouldn't marry him. Even if he still wanted her. After everything he had done to John, it would hurt John too much, and besides, Emma couldn't stand that man. On top of everything, it still didn't feel right to marry someone for money anyway. Deep down, she had always known that no matter how big of an ass William Blackwell was, it still didn't give her a moral get-out-of-jail-free card to use him as it pleased her.

"It is what it is." Emma would find a way back home. It might take a lifetime in poverty, but she would find a way home or die trying. She owed it to Lily and to herself. But first, she had to find a way to survive. And that wasn't quite so easy, considering where she was headed right now.

"Faster, you vazey cow," the filthy overseer shouted up at Emma, who was standing on a platform next to a big, round metal container full of boiling water.

Emma still wasn't sure what role the container played in the production of cloth, but she assumed it was cleaning the cloth before selling it. Emma picked up another big piece of white cotton and threw it in with the other fabrics. She then stirred it with a huge wooden stick, as if she was making an enormous pot of soup. Her hands were covered in blisters that wouldn't heal, thanks to working at this damn cotton factory every day from dusk until dawn. And every day meant *every day*. No Saturday or Sunday off. Not just a few overtime hours here or there on salary.

No. Every day meant every day, sunup to sundown.

Never had she worked so hard in her life. She bore a constant feeling of exhaustion, no matter the time of day. Heck, she even felt exhausted in her sleep! The first three weeks of working at the factory had been the hardest. She would constantly fall asleep, causing her to burn herself on the hot metal container several times a day. Every inch of her body hurt from torn muscles, blisters, burn marks, or exhaustion.

But she still preferred this to what poor Lily had to endure. Building up a new clientele in her line of work meant weeding out the "decent" from the abusive perverts. One night, Lily came home with a blue eye and a bleeding lip. Skip and Emma were so furious, they looked for that guy all night but never found him.

It had been over four months since Skip had woken Emma up in the middle of the night to lead her into this new chapter of her life. A chapter full of misery and pain. Lily and Emma had had to start fresh in a part of town where nobody knew them. William's private detective turned out to be quite good at his work, so they were always on the run. Skip was absolutely invaluable in helping them stay hidden. Lily had never told her what kind of work Skip was involved in, but she assumed it was something not entirely in agreement with the law, as he'd had to hide out a few times before and knew the ins and outs of how to be successful at it.

The dresses and jewelry Emma had received from William were the only reason they were not in the poorhouse yet. They had traded some of them for a room and food and other essential items. Still, the number of dresses was limited, so both Emma and Lily had had to go back to work to live from penny to penny, always just enough money to cover rent and have a little food in their stomachs.

Like an angel's voice from heaven, Emma heard that familiar bell ring, telling her and the rest of the burnt-out factory workers that another day in hell had just come to an end. People walked out of the factory like zombies, limping home in different directions. Emma looked up to the factory's entrance gate to see the familiar face she looked for every day. There she was. Like every evening, Lily was waiting for her, watching Emma's coworkers in disbelief.

"Why will you not try for another position? Somewhere else? Not even I would work at this death mill," Lily said to Emma the moment she arrived at the big, rusty metal gate. Emma hated that gate so much, she sometimes had nightmares about it.

"It's too risky. You know William and John are still asking around. It wouldn't be wise doing anything that would require me to talk a lot and expose my accent. This is fine, Lily. At least it's warm next to that damn pot."

Lily grabbed Emma's arm and turned it to get a better look at the latest burn she had brought back from the factory. The souvenir was a nasty one, and Emma was seriously worried about getting an infection from it.

"Really cozy," Lily countered sarcastically, holding Emma's arm up like evidence in court.

Emma was too tired to argue with her. They had been such a comfort to each other, and without Lily, Emma would probably have been dead somewhere in the streets, but lately, they argued a lot about the same things. Emma knew that Lily only meant well, so she wasn't really mad at her for continually trying to talk her into applying for different jobs, but Emma was worried about attracting attention and leading John or William or both right to them.

Skip reported on their efforts to find Emma regularly. According to Skip, nothing about the faked robbery had surfaced, and the police were not involved—yet—but who knew what William was up to? A man like William was capable of anything. Emma's best guess was revenge.

Then there was John. Kind, caring John. Every minute Emma was not in pain, she was thinking of his gentle smile, the one that always warmed her from the inside like a beautiful summer evening. Emma couldn't figure out why John was even looking for her. She couldn't see him craving revenge like William, so what did he want? Was he still in love with her, after everything she had done to him? It didn't matter. Let him find a woman he deserved. A woman who would not drag his family through a scandal.

"Come on, Lily, let's make our rounds," Emma said, disheartened, shaking off the thought of John.

Lily agreed, nodding her head quietly, but it was apparent she wasn't happy about dropping the subject of Emma working herself to death.

Emma gathered the tiny bit of energy that she'd kept hidden from that filthy, monstrous overseer who stalked around, beating on and yelling at the women to make them work faster. She hated him. Emma had never hated someone as much as that man. He was always covered in dirt and smelled awful.

One time, he'd had the audacity to swing that whip of his at Emma, hitting her right on the cheek. She had only stopped stirring the pot for a few seconds before he hit her, and by God, she would rather die than let some filthy man beat her up with a whip like she was some animal. She'd grabbed it out of his hands and swiped it right over that ugly face of his. It had cost her a full week's wage, but to Emma, it had been worth every penny. Seeing that whip smack that filthy smile right off his face had no price tag. After that, he had never touched her again, knowing that she would take him down right then and there, until her last breath if need be, should he ever lay hands on her.

After her shift at the factory of horrors, Emma and Lily would make their rounds visiting every pharmacy and drug store in London. Emma was trying hard to get everything she needed to make penicillin. About two years ago, she had learned how to make it in her college chemistry class; it was really not that hard to reproduce, if she could gather the ingredients. Many people didn't know it, but the main ingredient for penicillin was found at every corner: bread. Penicillin was made out of moldy bread. But things got a bit harder gathering the rest of what she would need, especially zinc sulfate.

For weeks, Emma and Lily had been running around London, trading dresses or jewelry for items on Emma's list. Lily wasn't entirely convinced that making penicillin was worth spending all of their savings, which was how she referred to William's gifts that now kept them aloft, but Emma had anticipated this kind of resistance from someone who didn't understand the concept of infections and antibiotics. To Emma, there was no doubt in her mind that the horrendous conditions of the slums they were living in would be her end before Christmas came around. Her body was not used to Victorian germs and poor hygienic standards, and even something as small as a scratch, or burn, could get infected and kill her in a matter of weeks.

She stood at the corner, watching Lily enter the drug store. The store was at the east end of town, and they had walked for two hours to get there. A different shop had referred them to it, stating that the guy there made all his drugs himself. It was Emma's last hope to get the final ingredient she needed. She stared at the store as if she was trying to hypnotize it. She would know in a matter of seconds if Lily had been successful or not, as Lily always smiled when she was successful—and there she was, exiting the pharmacy, giving Emma a cheerful smile. She couldn't believe it! She had everything together now to make penicillin! Much to Emma and Lily's surprise, Emma even found the energy to do a happy little jump.

"I can't believe it. They had it!" Emma shouted, grabbing the bag filled with the white powder out of Lily's hands.

"It was incredibly expensive. I do hope it is really that important."

"It is, Lily. Believe me." Emma felt a glimmer of hope for the first time in months. Now she had the means to stay alive longer by fighting the number one killer of the time—infection.

CHAPTER 11

"Fifty years ago, they would have called you a witch," Lily said, watching Emma move between several different-shaped glasses. In a matter of weeks, their room had gone from being empty to being stuffed with primitive lab equipment.

"Fifty years from now, the man who invents this will make history with one of the most important discoveries for mankind," Emma replied, holding a glass with moldy bread against the daylight shining in from the window. The mold had turned green, exactly what Emma needed. As crazy as it was, it was nothing more than mold on the dirty dishes of a researcher called Fleming that had led to the discovery of antibiotics in 1928.

Emma walked over to the windowsill to get the sterilized milk bottles that were filled with a simple solution of different salts and minerals. She had to separate the penicillin from the fungus today, so she would miss another day of work at the factory, but this was more important. Penicillin could save her from typhoid fever, syphilis, pneumonia, meningitis, common infections — the list was endless.

"If this can really cure all these diseases, then why do you not make plenty of it and then we can sell it?"

Emma had already thought of that herself. From cola to plastic, her options for inventing something would be endless.

"The number one rule of time travel, Lily. Remember…" Emma said as she mixed the green mold spores with the solution in one of the sterilized milk bottles.

"Do not change the course of history," Lily said, rolling her eyes.

By now, they were both totally comfortable talking about Emma's time travel. They had spent many nights turning on Emma's cell phone for just a few moments, looking at pictures. Emma allowed herself that luxury whenever she was about to give up. Whenever her hopes and dreams were crushed all over again by another day of living in poverty in Victorian London.

She repeated the step with all six of the milk bottles before turning to Lily.

"Don't change the temperature of the room. Leave the window closed and don't open any of those bottles for at least seven days," she said in a serious tone.

"Seven days? Has your nose adjusted to that fat overseer of yours so well that you cannot smell the stench of this house any longer?" Lily protested.

And rightfully so. The stench of the house they were renting a room in was terrible. A matching companion to everything else disgusting going on in the neighborhood they lived in. The roads were always wet and filled with a mixture of mud and feces, and it smelled like urine no matter where she went. Thieves and drunk fools filled the streets night and day alike, and dirty children without shoes begged in front of the houses, including the one Emma and Lily lived in.

"I know. I'm sorry. I'll trade another dress today. We are out of money again anyway. I'll grab a cheap perfume so we will survive the seven days with a closed window without getting nauseous."

That seemed to persuade Lily a bit. Emma went to the dresser and grabbed the blue dress she'd worn at William's hunting party. She was kind of glad to see that one go. Emma put it in a sack used for carrying potatoes so nobody would see the dress and follow her to rob her in some shady alley. All of this was part of her reality now.

"Do not forget to get some more bread too. Your penicillin or whatever you call it is eating all of ours."

Emma headed out to the pawnshop a few blocks down the street. It was a terrible rip-off place, but the owner was one of the very few to never ask where the items people brought to his shop came from. Emma would have to come up with a different way of making money soon, as there were only two items left to trade after this fine blue dress was gone. One was a hat, and the other one…the nightgown she had worn all those months ago when she and John made love. Emma was holding on to it for as long as she could. Sometimes, when she couldn't sleep, she would walk over to the dresser and hold that nightgown close to her heart, breathing in John's smell, which still lingered on it like a distant memory.

Emma was torn out of her bittersweet daydreams by a dirty hand slamming a few coins onto the counter in front of her. The pawnshop's owner was a skinny, bald man who reminded Emma of a reptile. His shop was dark and stuffed with dusty items, a fitting home for a slimy snake, Lily always said.

"He ye go, lass." He grinned, revealing rotten teeth. Emma wanted to take the money, but he didn't remove his hand, trapping the coins underneath it. His breath was horrendous as he leaned in closer to add, "Ye know, a pretty lass lek you do no hav to be walkin' ve streets all alone."

Emma reached in her skirt's pocket, slowly pulling out a knife. "I'm not alone. My little friend here keeps me company wherever I go," she threatened him in a low voice.

He let go of the coins and folded the dress Emma had just traded as though he'd never said a thing. "Just sein, lass."

"Me too," she replied, taking the coins. The money the snake paid this time was not even a tenth of what he should have paid for the dress, but she had no choice but to take whatever he offered. Emma kept the knife out all the way to the pawn shop's door, holding it like a shield.

Finally out, she slammed the door behind herself, cursing loudly.

"I assume you are as good with a knife as you are with a pistol," a familiar voice said.

Emma felt an icy shiver run down her spine. She recognized the voice immediately. There was only one person with such a deep and manly voice, and under different circumstances, she would have called it sexy. She didn't want to believe it, but there he was. The Duke of Davenport, William Blackwell, in all his handsome but hideously arrogant glory.

Emma had been preparing for this moment for months, but her body still did its own thing, and she dropped her coins onto the street in shock the moment she set eyes on him. Beggars rushed to Emma's feet, snatching the coins up like fish launching at little breadcrumbs. She just stood there, watching her meal for the months ahead disappear along with the people who stole it. *Let them have it*, she thought. She wouldn't give William the pleasure of seeing her on her knees, fighting over pennies.

"There is only one way to find out," Emma now commented in that same threatening voice.

William laughed. He was standing in front of a fancy carriage with a big, golden "B" on the side of it. A man stood right next to the carriage, making it clear that he belonged to William.

"There is no need for that, Emma. I have no desire to hurt you. If that was my intention, I would not be standing here in front of you."

He was right—this was not what revenge would look like. Emma put the knife away.

"It is good to see that poverty did not break your spirit. Not yet, at least."

Emma took a few steps closer to him. "What do you want, William?" She crossed her arms across her chest.

"To talk. I just want to talk to you." He opened the door to his carriage. Emma didn't move.

"I see you brought your dog," she said in a condescending tone, nodding in the direction of the man who was standing close to the carriage. He must have been in his sixties, and although not dressed poorly, he was clearly not part of society.

"Quite the opposite. He brought me," William said calmly. "But have it your way. You will not be needed any longer, Gustav," William told

Gustav, who turned around and disappeared down a side street like a ghost who had never been there at all. William turned back to Emma. "Just you and me now. See?"

"We can talk here."

William tilted his head to the side. "If you want to, but it might attract some attention when we get to the interesting parts, such as the fake robbery." He grinned, knowing he had her.

Although she hated it, William held all the cards. She had no choice but to go with him and see what he had to say. Causing a scene right here wouldn't help anybody, especially considering the circumstances.

"Well?" William stretched out his hand to offer to help her into the carriage. Emma walked straight by him, getting into the carriage without saying a word or taking his hand. William followed her with his big, smug grin. The carriage took off.

William opened a trunk that was on the floor and pulled out a dress. He placed it next to Emma.

"You might want to put that on before we get to my townhouse," he said, analyzing her from head to toe.

"I'm not planning on going to your townhouse with you. Say what you have to say, and I will be on my way again."

"Very well. Then let us begin with the robbery you staged. Oh, please do tell me about that..."

Emma didn't even try to think of an excuse. There was no use creating more fairytales. William had probably already gathered evidence he could use against her at any time.

She sighed. "What do you want to know?"

"Why you did it. The how is not needed. I already figured that part out."

Emma looked straight at him now. "Money."

"What for?"

This question surprised Emma. William was smarter than she thought. He seemed to know her well enough to realize that she didn't care about money in and of itself.

"Research."

"Research?" William drew his brows together in confusion.

Like always, Emma followed the most crucial rule of lying: stay as close to the truth as possible to make it believable. "Yes. I didn't plan to end up in England. In order for me to resolve the issue that got me here in the first place, I needed to figure out a way how to do that. For that, I needed time and access to educational facilities. Something the jobs in the slums do not come with."

William looked deep into her eyes, as if he could find the truth in them. "To be clear, you acquired the help of a gambler and a wagtail to stage a robbery to swindle me into marrying you, so you could have the money and freedom you needed to leave me whenever you found a way back home?"

Emma hadn't known that Skip was a gambler, but it didn't matter at this point. It sounded pretty bad when he said it like that. Emma felt ashamed. Sure, William was a douche, but she was better than that. The whole situation was a shit show, and the worst part about it was the fact that John had been dragged into it.

Emma looked down at the floor. It was evident that William wouldn't let her get away with this charade. Maybe she could beg him to leave Lily and Skip out of it. Tell him it was all her idea, and they had no idea what they were getting into. It really was all her fault anyway, so she should take the fall alone.

Suddenly, William burst out in uproarious laughter. Emma stared at him in disbelief. Had he gone mad?

"Marvelous! Emma, you are truly amazing!" William wheezed between heaving breaths. He had tears in his eyes from laughing.

"Wait…what?" She was totally lost.

"I have never met a woman like you. Truth is, I have never met *anybody* like you. The craziest part about all of this is that it would have worked if that filthy thief had not come forward to tell Gustav about you. You would have gotten away with it. Fooled me into marrying you. Played me like a fiddle." William's laughter slowly died down, but he was still smiling.

Emma just stared at him, unable to think of anything to say to that.

"Nobody has ever managed to do that, Emma. You truly are my equal."

Emma was far from feeling flattered. She was too busy trying to figure out what William could possibly want from her. So far, it didn't sound like he would have her thrown in jail, so what was he planning?

"I am afraid I don't understand what's going on," Emma stated carefully.

William became serious. "You see, Emma, the thing is that you set out to make me marry you. And I intend to do so."

Wait…what? Had she heard that right? After everything that had happened, William still wanted to marry her? Why?

"You must be joking."

"I am dead serious. I never thought I would find my equal, a partner who would challenge me, interest me, attract me…" William now threw a more sensual look at her. "But I guess I did not find you. You found me."

As twisted as this all was, Emma started to see the logic behind William's words. He wasn't in love with her. He didn't want her because of who she was. To William, she was nothing more than the biggest challenge of his life. He needed to possess her so she would entertain him like a clown.

She would rather live a life of poverty than be his personal comedian. Besides, she could never do this to John.

"I can't marry you, William. I'm sorry. And before you start blackmailing me, just take a look at me. Do I look like I have anything left to lose?" Emma laughed sarcastically. She must have looked awful, dressed in rags, unwashed, and full of burn marks on her arms.

A shimmer of anger flared up in his eyes. "I was afraid you would say that. This has to do with that fool, Evergreen, doesn't it?"

Emma stopped laughing. William took this as a confession.

"Bloody hell, do not be so absurd. Evergreen is no match for you. I am surprised he even looked for you for as long as he did, but then, he also doesn't know what a cunning woman he brought into his house. Thought he was protecting your honor when, in reality, he was the one who needed protection." William raised a confident brow at her, his fingers steepled in front of him.

Emma knew exactly what he was implying here.

"So, you didn't tell him anything?" she asked, just to confirm his intentions.

"And drag him and his family through the same misery they already had to endure all those years ago? Poor Evergreen would have to join the military for life to restore his family's name after your scandal came to light. An affair with an impersonator...way worse than the rumors brokenhearted Elise spread back then."

Finally. William had gotten to the point. If Emma didn't agree to marry him, he would tell John all about Emma and expose her in public, causing a scandal for the Evergreens. William knew what he was doing.

"A marriage between the two of us will not make him happy, of course, but with his name still spotless, he would get over it at some point. Still better than not getting the girl *and* seeing his family in ruin. A lesser-evil situation of some sort. But, of course, it is all up to you, dear Emma." William knocked against the ceiling. The carriage stopped. "You can leave now or put on that dress and come with me to announce our engagement to my family and society."

Emma glared at him silently. She felt her heart filling with anger like never before. But then, if she was to hate someone, it should be herself. She was the one who had started all of this, challenged William into marrying her. This was simply the end result of her own actions. Emma's ability to find a positive in even the worst circumstances seemed to have gone on vacation, as there was nothing but sadness and anger in her heart right now. Emma didn't say a word. Didn't move. She felt tears brewing but swallowed them down. She wouldn't give William the satisfaction of seeing her cry.

He opened the door as is if to say, *"Here you go,"* but Emma stayed.

"That is what I thought. Good girl." He closed the door again. "Now, please put on that dress and look happy. We do not want anybody to think I just picked you up in one of London's worst parts of town looking like a factory girl."

CHAPTER 12

John read the line again and again and again. His mother had brought him the newspaper today, something which was odd in itself. Now he knew why. He reread the sentence once more just to make sure. His mother and sister were standing behind him.

"John… I am so sorry…" his mother said in a tone so soft it was nearly a whisper.

John put the newspaper down and got up. "About what?" he said with a fake smile. He kissed his mother on her cheek. "There is nothing to worry about, Mother."

John walked out of the breakfast room with fast, determined steps. He caught his mother and sister exchanging concerned looks as he went by them. As blind as they had been about his feelings for Emma before, hearing John shout that night, begging Emma to open her door, had made it very clear to them both, and the rest of the house, that he loved her.

John opened the door to his office and walked straight to the large mahogany desk. He poured himself a glass of brandy from a whiskey tray and pounded it down in one fluid motion. He then rang a bell for the butler.

Penley opened the door and stepped in. "You called, my lord?"

"Yes, please call my solicitor. I want to see him."

"Of course, your lordship." Penley did a courtesy bow and closed the door behind himself.

John gazed over the newspaper one more time, reading the headline again:

Engagement Announcement. The Duke of Davenport is to be married to Mrs. Emma Washington.

He threw the newspaper carelessly onto the desk, watching a few of the pages fall onto the floor. He poured himself another glass and pounded that one down as well. His heart felt that familiar stabbing pain again. Something he had to endure every time he thought of Emma, ever since the night she disappeared. All she'd left behind was a note that arrived the next day, saying nothing more than thanks for his hospitality and not to blame himself.

For months, he had been looking for her. He had employed several private detectives who all came back with different information. One of them had reported that Davenport was looking for her as well, and that a man named Flinch knew something about her but had disappeared after talking to Davenport's hound, Gustav. The only other breakthrough he'd had was finding out that Emma's maid Lily was a prostitute in the same part of town John had spent countless nights trying to save veterans in need.

That was all he had left of her. Rumors and a short note. Actually, that wasn't true. There was still that ridiculous announcement put out by Davenport shortly after Emma's disappearance, stating that she had gone back to America to make certain arrangements, hinting at an engagement. John had thought it was nonsense, but why openly get into it with Davenport when he didn't even know where Emma was himself?

He'd often wondered if this was all his fault. Love or not, he had taken advantage of her, so who could blame her for running away from him? By God, he couldn't even blame her for marrying the duke. He had been more of a gentleman in all of this than John had been. He just wished he could have seen her one more time, to apologize, give her whatever she asked of him. Anything and everything. But none of that mattered any longer. The woman he loved would marry William Blackwell. What a fitting end to a drama that had played its first act over ten years ago.

John sat down behind his desk just to stand up again. He couldn't sit still and wait around for his solicitor. He would ride to him instead. If John knew one thing for sure, it was that his time at Evergreen had come to an end as well. He would sell. This time, without hesitation. John knew that he wouldn't be able to bear living next to Emma, Duchess of Davenport, running into her on carriage rides and neighborhood gatherings.

No, he would move. Far away. Maybe Ireland? Or Italy? He smiled sarcastically at the thought of himself becoming the second person Davenport had sent on the run to Italy. If it weren't for Emma, he would have challenged Davenport to a duel. But how could he do that to her after everything she'd had to endure? He couldn't, was the answer. John pounded another glass of brandy before making haste out of the office and into the entrance hall.

"Somebody get my horse ready! Now!" John shouted, so unlike his usual calm self.

Ten years, he had played with the idea of selling Evergreen Castle so he would never have to deal with Davenport again. The man was like a wildfire, leaving behind a trail of destruction and ashes. The list of heartbroken women was so long that society didn't even care anymore when another name was added to it.

But if Emma wanted to get married to Davenport, he would respect her choice. For months, he had been trying to find her, to talk to her...but quite clearly, she didn't want to be found. At least, not by him. John would do the right thing and leave her be, even if that was the hardest, most painful thing he had ever had to do.

Emma's footsteps echoed through the mighty entrance hall. It was so loud, it hurt her ears. She was dressed in the finest Chinese silk London had to offer. Her light-pink gown looked stunning on her, and the trail behind her dress was a bit longer than what she was used to but fitting for a Blackwell. Future Duchess of Davenport. She passed by the drawing room but stopped as soon as she saw Winston, the townhome's butler.

"Winston, what happened to the rugs I bought for the entrance hall? Walking on that darn marble echoes so loudly. It makes my ears hurt." It really did. At first, she didn't want to say anything, but Emma had been in and out so many times, she would suffer from hearing loss walking on this floor if somebody didn't put a rug in here soon.

"I am sorry, my lady, but the current Duchess of Davenport had them removed again. She said these floors are the most expensive part of the house and should not be hidden under cheap rugs."

Emma rolled her eyes. Since she arrived at William's townhome about a month ago, his mother and sister had fought her every chance they got. They were outspoken about their disapproval of the pending marriage, and despite William laying out the law for them, they would not give up quite so easily.

"I saw poor Nancy cover her ears in pain from these floors the other day. Are we living in a cave here?" Emma responded, annoyed with the Blackwells.

It was true. Poor Nancy, one of the maids, had had to clean that entrance hall earlier in the week, and for hours she'd had to endure the loud echoes of footsteps.

Winston looked at her as if he was caught between enemy lines.

"No worries, Winston." Emma turned around and headed toward her room upstairs.

Like everything in this house, her room was decorated in gold and the finest fabrics and paintings in the country. Emma didn't have time for this battle of rugs. She was working day and night trying to find a way back home. If she could manage to figure out what had happened to her before her scheduled wedding day in April, she could get out of here without ever having to get married to William. Luckily enough, it was Blackwell tradition to marry on the day the very first Blackwell was called into aristocracy by the King of England—April the 5th. That gave her a few months to figure things out.

William was keeping a close eye on her but wasn't too concerned about her running away again, as he had made it very clear that he would simply find her again. Emma couldn't care less; her next attempt at running away would be back into the future, and there was no way he would find her in a different century. So Emma didn't give two cents about his threats or constant surveillance and did her research in the open. By now, Emma was so used to Gustav stalking her, she almost felt weird when he wasn't following her.

Emma walked into her bathroom, which she had slowly transformed into a small lab. One of the few rooms neither Gustav nor William stepped foot into. Lily was in there, mixing the solution that was needed to separate penicillin spores from mold. After Emma had used her homemade penicillin and successfully cured her infected arm and one of Lily's coworkers who suffered from a horrendous case of syphilis, Lily had developed quite an interest in chemistry.

"How was your meeting with the witches?" Lily asked with an ironic grin on her face.

She was dressed in clothes far too fine for a maid. Emma had fought William tooth and nail over letting Lily stay with her. At first, he was totally against it but had finally given in after Emma threatened to call off the wedding if William wouldn't save Lily from the poorhouse. Lily now helped Emma with odd tasks that could assist Emma in her quest to find a way out of 1881.

"It was ridiculous. They were talking about creating spells using cat urine and baby poop, but when I asked about time travel, they looked at me as if I was totally out of my mind." Emma sat down on the edge of the bathtub and sighed.

She had chased down several promising leads, but all of them had resulted in dead ends. Just like the one today. She had found out one thing, though—that darn coin, the very reason for Emma getting hit by that car in the first place, had turned out to be nothing more than a typical Victorian shilling, found at every street corner. The disappointment Emma felt when she had learned that was beyond imaginable. But what had she hoped to find out? That this coin was, in fact, some magical coin with great powers, like Frodo's precious ring in *Lord of the Rings*?

The clock struck eight, and Emma looked up at Lily, who stopped mixing powders and caught Emma's stare with empathy.

"Why do you not tell him that you are feeling under the weather?" Lily asked.

Emma thought about it for a second but shook her head. "I don't want to push him. If he gets nothing in return and grows tired of us, he might ruin us after all, or worse."

217

Lily knew exactly what that meant. Flinch was still nowhere to be found, and Lily and Emma were growing more and more suspicious that William had something to do with his mysterious disappearance. No, Emma had to go. This was the only thing William asked of her right now, to join him every evening at eight in the library for drinks and conversation. He had even stuck to his promise to wait until they were wed before expecting her to share his bed, so far. Still, Emma dreaded those evenings in the library in his company, always walking on eggshells, never knowing what he would do or want next. She was like a doll that he could take out to play with and put away whenever it pleased him.

William was already sitting in one of the chairs next to the gigantic marble fireplace when Emma joined him. The flames within were flickering strongly, sending warmth and a cozy light into the room. William was sipping on a glass of whiskey.

"There you are. Whiskey?"

"Yes, please," Emma said, sitting down across from him on a lounge chair.

William walked over to a little liquor table that offered several choices of the finest brands in town. He poured Emma a glass of the Irish whiskey she liked so much and handed it to her.

"Thanks."

William sat down across from her again. Like every night, he started to talk about a topic of his interest. Emma only heard the beginning; something about the stock market in America was the last thing Emma processed before drifting off, thinking of John. That was something she did quite often, especially when sitting in the library. She remembered their passionate lovemaking in his room, in front of a fireplace similar to the one she was sitting next to right now, just a lot smaller. She felt the usual tingle in her stomach when she thought about how gently John had kissed her, entered her. The beautiful feeling was soon to be replaced with an overwhelming sadness. She missed him so much. What was he up to? Was he still thinking of her? Or did he hate her?

"Emma!" William pulled her back into the current moment.

She blinked at him, unsure how long he had been talking.

"You are doing it again," he said, rolling his eyes.

"I'm sorry. It has been a long day, and I'm tired." Emma stood up to signal that she would like to retire.

William took a sip from his whiskey, leaning his head to the side as he pondered whether he should let her go or not.

"Not yet," he determined. "Sit back down and tell me about your day. You attended a lecture by that insane scientist, did you not? Tesla?"

William had no idea that the crazy scientist was one of the greatest minds of all time. It was a long shot, but Emma was toying with the idea that electricity could have something to do with her situation. Heck, she'd traveled back in time. Her plan to attend a Tesla lecture and ask a few targeted questions was making far more sense than that meeting with the witches had. If Emma remembered correctly, Tesla and Edison were just about to start their War of Currents within the next year or so.

"No, that isn't until the end of next month. Today, I was trapped for six hours in a ceremony with a bunch of old women who thought they could make someone fall in love by using cat urine."

William threw his head back and slapped his leg, laughing wholeheartedly. "I hope you took some of it and thought of me," he said, gasping for air.

"Nope. Sorry. I tried to leave five minutes into it, but they wouldn't let me. Those damn fools said I would mess with the energy flow if I left early, so they locked me in with them." Emma crossed her arms, something she did a lot in William's presence.

William barely got a hold of himself. "Really, Emma, my life was quite boring before you came along."

Every night, she had to amuse William like a court jester. She had to remind herself that this wouldn't last forever, or she would sail into total despair like a ship lost at sea.

"I'm glad I entertain you so much," she said with a hint of annoyance.

"Oh, do not get angry. I am just enjoying myself a bit. So, when will you tell me what this is really all about? Witches, mad scientists, all those mysterious daily rounds. What are you trying to accomplish?"

"Why don't you ask Gustav? He's there with me every step of the way." Emma finished her drink.

"I have a feeling that poor Gustav does not have the slightest inclination about what you are really doing. But, for now, we can keep it this way. I am entertained enough by how things stand."

Emma got out of her chair and put her empty glass on a little table close to it. William didn't stop her this time, which meant he would let her go now. He stood up and leaned in to give her the usual goodnight kiss on the cheek. Emma hated his touch but had no choice but to let it happen.

"Well, I cannot wait to hear about your next adventure tomorrow," William said, opening the door for Emma. She stepped out into the hallway.

"Tomorrow, then," she said, heading back to her room, leaving behind the loud echoes of footsteps on cold marble floors.

This was her life. Amusing some entitled duke in Victorian London. Soon, she would have to entertain him in other ways as well. The thought of having to sleep with him made her gag.

She had to find a way out. Double her efforts. Tomorrow, she would go back to the library and talk to the old man who worked there. He knew a thing or two about who was what in London, and Emma wanted to see if he knew of any people who specialized in the study of time.

Like so many nights before, she lay in bed awake, thinking of John. What was he doing? He knew now where to find her. Would he come and talk to her? Insist he still loved her and take her away? Emma tossed herself to her side.

It must have been barely past ten when Emma heard that familiar light knock against her window. Lily, who had been sleeping on a chaise lounge, got up and opened it.

"This Davenport gentleman is making it incredibly hard to get to yer," Skip said, climbing into the room. He walked straight to the fire and sat down next to it, starting to eat the sandwich and sausage from the plate Emma had waiting for him every night.

"Still no match for Skip the Wise," he grinned, then took a big bite from the sausage.

Skip had become family to Emma. Like Lily, Emma wouldn't be alive if it wasn't for him. He'd watched out for both Lily and Emma when they'd had to hide in the roughest parts of London. He taught her how to use the knife she always carried no matter where she went. Now, he was helping with errands that William and his hound Gustav didn't need to know about. Mostly gathering substances for making medications and snooping into William's daily activities. William wasn't the only one who thought it wise to keep an eye on people. Thanks to Skip's efforts, Emma had been able to make aspirin, and find out that William's only real interests next to Emma were horses and guns. He was one of the best shots in the country, something not very comforting to know.

"Anything interesting today?" Like every night, she was hoping to hear from John.

"Interestin', indeed. Good, certainly not," Skip said, putting the food down. "They found Flinch."

Emma and Lily both jumped up in anticipation. "What? Where? Is he all right? Did he say anything?"

Skip opened the beer bottle and took a long pull from it. "Flinch will not say a word ter nobody ever again. They found him in the Thames. People think he bragged too loudly about his coins, so someone robbed and killed him."

Emma and Lily looked at each other, knowing they were thinking the same thing.

"Or someone killed him to keep him quiet about Emma."

Skip thought about it for a second. "Why would someone do that?"

"To avoid a scandal and keep her under that someone's complete control."

This took things to a whole new level. Flinch was gone, most likely killed by the very man who already dictated her life like a puppet master. Not that Emma felt bad for Flinch. Skip assured her that he was the lowest form of life to have ever inhabited this earth. But now, Emma would never be able to question him, find out what had happened before he tried to rob her the day she woke up in the street.

"But that is not all, is it?" Lily announced, more a statement than a question.

Emma turned toward him again.

"Don' know what yer mean," Skip said, scratching his nose and avoiding her gaze.

"There…you are scratching your nose," Lily accused him, trapping him between the fireplace and herself.

Skip had a bad tell whenever he lied or hid something from people he cared about. He turned around and held his hands up, warming them innocently over the comforting warmth of the fire.

"I don' know what yor talkin' about."

Emma walked straight up to him and spun him around.

"Skip, you know how much it worries me when you do that. Is something the matter with you? Are you sick?" Emma was deeply concerned now.

He looked at her for a second, then finally gave in. "It would be better if yer don't know, Emma."

"Please…tell me," she said, grabbing his shoulders.

Skip took a deep breath in and exhaled it rapidly. "Very well, but please promise me you will not do anythin' foolish."

"I'll try," she promised.

"Evergreen…"

Emma's eyes widened in shock as she started to shake him. "What is it? Is he all right? Tell me!"

Skip grabbed both of Emma's hands and held them close together.

"John Evergreen is fine, but his mother…she is dying of the cough."

Emma stumbled a few steps back. An icy shiver ran through her entire body like a raging blizzard. The cough that Skip was referring to was Victorian English for pneumonia.

"But how is that possible?! She was perfectly fine the last time I saw her!" Emma shook her head in disbelief.

Skip scratched his head. "These sorts of things can happen out of nowhere. I am sure yer know that better than I do."

He was right, anything could have been the cause, especially in a time with such low medical standards. Emma thought of John. He must have been going through pure hell right now. Couldn't life just cut him a break? Emma grabbed a bag and rushed into the bathroom. Skip and Lily followed her.

"You said yer would not do anything foolish," Skip protested.

Emma grabbed a bottle of penicillin and put it in the bag. "I said I would try."

Lily blocked her way out. "Skip is right. If William finds out about you rushing to John Evergreen in the middle of the night, who knows what he would do to all of us. Evergreens included."

Emma gently pushed her out of the way. "You know that I can't just let Lady Evergreen die," Emma said and began getting changed into the pink dress she had worn earlier.

Skip turned around to give her some privacy.

"At least wait until the morning. Maybe the duke will allow you to go." Lily sounded concerned, and rightfully so. William was capable of anything.

"I can't. At her age, every hour counts. She might be dead in the morning. If I leave now, I could make it back before the servants get up.

William might never find out," Emma said, determined.

Lily put on her shoes.

"What are you doing?"

"I am coming with you."

"No, Lily. You can't. If William should find out, he won't unleash his anger on both of us if only I go."

"You're talking a load of cobblers. I can cop a mouse if things go wrong and you shouldn't be wasting time arguing with me. If we leave now, we can be back before dawn. I cannot let you go alone, and you know that. It is not safe for a lady alone in the dark. Even if that lady is Emma Washington."

Emma knew Lily too well. She wouldn't give in. She looked over to Skip, who was already climbing out the window.

"Let me guess, you are coming as well?"

"You're a woman after my heart, so of course I'm coming."

Emma let out a long, audible breath before she followed Skip down his self-made, foldable, very unstable ladder. She felt bad for dragging them into this, but at the same time, it made her truly happy that she had two friends who cared for her so deeply and had her back no matter what. No, they weren't friends. They were family.

CHAPTER 13

Emma's heart started pounding wildly against her chest the moment the carriage pulled up in front of the Evergreen estate. It was dark and quiet out, and she could barely see the entrance door. Emma hadn't thought that she would ever be able to step foot into this home again. It didn't have marble floors and extravagant golden decor in every room like all of William's residences, but Emma had a feeling of belonging here. Besides, it was still a stunning castle.

Skip had gotten the carriage from a merchant who was willing to be discreet about the late-night ride for a few extra coins. Emma stepped out of it and turned around to look at Lily and Skip.

"We shall wait for you here," Lily whispered.

Emma understood why they were giving her privacy. The conversation with John might turn ugly, so it would be better if she could have it under only four eyes, not eight.

The door opened before Emma could knock. Penley was staring into her face with a mixture of curiosity and disbelief.

"Mrs. Washington?!"

He walked her into the entrance hall.

"Penley, would you be so kind as to give this to Lord Evergreen or Agnes, please?" Emma asked, grabbing the little bottle of penicillin out of her purse.

"That will not be necessary, Penley. She can hand it to me herself," said the voice Emma had craved to hear for so many months.

John was standing at the top of the stairs looking down at her. Penley waited for a few seconds to see if John had any other requests before he returned to sit down on a chair in the entrance hall.

Emma just stood there, looking at John. He looked so tired, as though he hadn't slept in months. His hair was falling loosely into his face, and his white shirt was unbuttoned halfway down his chest, exposing some of his scars.

"I have to admit, I did not think I would ever see you again, Mrs. Washington—or is it Duchess of Davenport yet?" he said in a cool tone, watching Emma as she walked up the first step of the stairway leading to the bedrooms on the first floor.

"John, I..." Emma lost her words. What was she supposed to say? It all looked terrible. He'd saved her from the side of the road, taken her into his home, welcomed her into his family. Then he had given her his loving heart, something he had never given a woman before. And what had Emma done in return? She had run away in the middle of the night, resurfacing months later engaged to his worst enemy, the Duke of Davenport. She wouldn't be surprised if he threw her out without letting her say one more word.

No, she had to give him the medication for his mother before he could do that. It was the very least she could do for the man she loved with all her heart.

Emma gathered all her courage and walked up the stairs. She stopped right in front of him and held up the bottle of penicillin.

"Give two tablespoons of this to your mother every four hours for ten days," Emma said, avoiding eye contact with John.

Much to her surprise, he took it without asking what it was.

"Ah, the miracle cure, I assume? Is that what they call it? So, you are the one curing all those prostitutes?"

Emma stared at him, completely shocked.

"I heard about this wonder cure from one of my fallen veterans, a regular at the brothels. I was looking everywhere to get ahold of one of these bottles, but not a single prostitute would talk to me. I am quite impressed with their loyalty."

That was bad news. Word of the cure seemed to have spread fast and far amongst the prostitutes and veterans. It was only a matter of time before it would lead to Emma if she and Lily continued to help people at this rate. Emma wanted to help these poor souls more than anything, but if things got out of control and led to the discovery of penicillin before 1928, it could change history as she knew it forever.

Emma looked down at the floor again. She couldn't bear looking at John's passionate brown eyes. They were just as beautiful as she remembered, bringing back memories of tender words whispered into her ear. Emma felt that all too familiar tingling in her stomach again.

"I just came to give you this. I better go." She turned around, ready to run back to the carriage, but John grabbed her by the wrist and spun her around again to face him.

"So, this is it? Are you going to leave just like that again? For months, I have been looking for you so I could apologize to you. Chasing every lead I could get. I was up day and night thinking about you, worried something might have happened to you. Hating myself for what I have done to you. And then I read in the newspaper that Mrs. Emma Washington is not only well but also is to marry William Blackwell, the biggest buffoon I have ever come across. And believe me, I have come across a lot of despicable people.

Nothing made sense anymore. I told myself that I just never really knew you. That you were not the person I thought you to be. God, I convinced myself of that so bloody well that I started to believe it. And now, here you are. In the middle of the night. Sneaking out on that monster of a fiancé to save my mother, along with half of London's prostitutes. You're a bricky girl, Emma. Just like the selfless person I always knew you were, the Emma I fell in love with—" John stopped talking abruptly, as if he'd said too much.

Emma looked at him for a moment but wasn't sure how to read his face. Was he still in love with her? After everything that had happened? *No. Impossible.*

Her eyes fell to her feet in shame. "John, you have done nothing to me. You saved me, showed me love. If anything, I'm the one who needs to beg for forgiveness."

John lifted her chin up to force her to look him in the eye. He did it softly, exactly the same way he used to before kissing her. But this time, he looked deep into her eyes, as if he were searching for the truth in them.

Emma wanted to kiss him more than she had ever wanted to kiss him before. But John was not hers to claim any longer. She tried to pull her arm out of his grip, which resulted in her coat sliding off her arm, exposing her scars from the clothing factory. John tightened his grip and pulled her arm closer to his face, turning it left and right to get a good look at the scars she was trying to hide.

"Jesus Christ, Emma. What the hell happened? Did Davenport do this to you? The meater! I shall kill him! I swear it!" John shouted angrily.

"No, he didn't. I had a few rough months after I left, that's all."

John appeared truly shocked by this new piece of information. He opened his mouth to say something, but the door to his mother's bedroom swung open, and Agnes came out.

"John, is something the matter?" Agnes asked, not realizing at first that Emma was with him. When she saw Emma, she yelped, "Dear goodness, Emma! What are you doing here?" Agnes came closer, holding her hands up to her face.

This was not good. She was supposed to just drop off the medication without being seen. If William found out about this...

Emma pulled herself free from John's grip.

"I have to go. I'm so, so sorry, John!" She took one last look at his beautiful face before escaping down the stairs and out the front door. She hurtled herself into the carriage and shouted at the driver to leave. Fiery tears were running down her face. She loved him. She loved him so much!

"Emma!" she heard John shouting, running after the carriage.

She yelled at the driver again, and he commanded the horses to go faster.

"Emmaaaaaaaa!" she heard him shouting again and again until the carriage pulled her too far away, silencing his voice in the dark night.

Lily took Emma into her arms, moving her hand slowly up and down Emma's back. "Please don't cry. It will get better...shh...it will get better," she softly said, desperately trying to comfort her.

But Emma cried aloud as she had never cried before. She had never felt love for anybody like she did for John. Her heart wasn't broken, it was destroyed beyond repair. Her cries didn't die down until her body was too weak to shed even one more tear.

You are a Washington, so you will live your life in misery, just like the rest of us. Her father's words kept running through her head again. She hated him just as much as she hated William. Two abusive men, making sure that the Washington curse would live on and on forever.

Emma woke up to the rumbling noises of servants moving things in the hallway. She had barely slept more than an hour, and even that one hour hadn't been peaceful, as she'd had a nightmare about falling into a dark hole.

Lily jumped out of bed as if she were ready to defend herself from attackers. She waited for a few seconds, then peeked out the door to see what was going on.

Emma could hear her exchange a few sentences with a servant before closing the door behind herself again. She turned to Emma, looking bewildered. "We are leaving!"

Now it was Emma's turn to jump out of bed. "We're *what*? To where?"

Emma rushed over to her dresser to throw on her morning robe. She stormed out to look for William, whom she found reading a newspaper in the breakfast room. He lowered it, as if he knew what was coming his way.

"Where are we going?" Emma asked in a demanding tone.

"Ah, good morning to you as well. To Italy." William's face disappeared back behind the newspaper, as though nothing was out of the ordinary. Like always, everything about him looked perfect, from his polished shoes to his dark, neatly styled hair.

"But why?" Emma asked, taking a few steps closer to him.

William didn't bother to lower his newspaper again. "Because it pleases me."

Emma didn't have to see his face to know that he was grinning. Emma clenched her fists. She was so angry, it took all of her strength to refrain from ripping that newspaper out of his hands and smacking that grin right off his face with it.

Sweet memories arose in her mind, of the time she had swiped another abusive man's smile right off his face with the very same whip he'd used to beat her. Back then, Emma had been dressed in rags and always one step away from the poorhouse, but she had been happier there than she ever was in William's golden cage. She walked over and pushed his newspaper down to reveal his face.

"I still have work here; I can't just leave."

William straightened his newspaper and folded it neatly. "You will be able to find witches and mad scientists in Rome as well," he said, flashing her an arrogant smile.

Emma clenched her fists a little tighter, inhaling sharply through her nose.

"And besides, it might help with your sleep problems. You seem to be up a lot lately."

Emma's anger turned to worry. Was he referring to last night? Did he know? Emma didn't know what to say. No, she knew of plenty of things to say to William, but none of them would end well for her. She had to think of John, Lily, and even Skip now, who was losing in cards a lot lately and relied on her to survive.

William got up. "Splendid. We shall leave around noon." He was already at the door when he turned around again. "Oh...and refresh yourself. You look terrible. Like a skilamalink! Embarrassing. Not like a Blackwell at all."

He closed the door behind himself, leaving Emma with a heart full of hatred. She was constantly on the brink of throwing in the towel, letting him ruin her and the Evergreens, going back to poverty or jail just to be free of him. But then, would she be free of him? At this point, there was even the chance of him doing far worse to her or John than ruin. If Lily and Skip were right, William was the reason Flinch had been floating in the Thames for months, barely recognizable when they finally found him.

Lily entered the breakfast room quietly. She looked as if she wanted to take Emma into her arms, but Emma took a step back.

"That won't be necessary, Lily. Everything is fine."

Lily seemed surprised at how cold Emma had sounded. Emma was surprised too. Was she at a breaking point? Turning into ice to protect her feelings? Would anger and hatred for William soon be the only emotions left in her heart? Emma was fine with that. At least it would cut her a break from the constant sadness that took over when she thought of John. She was a survivor. She wouldn't shed a single tear over this anymore. From now on, she would simply survive. Emma left the breakfast room to start packing, leaving behind a deeply troubled and worried Lily.

John was sitting at his mother's bedside when the door opened, and a servant brought in a letter on a silver tray. He looked at the note for a few seconds before taking it. Was it from Emma? He felt that heavy feeling in his heart again. He'd been up all night, thinking about her whenever he wasn't holding his mother's weak hand.

What had she been thinking, just showing up like that? If anybody besides Agnes or Penley had seen her, it would have ruined her reputation and ended her engagement to Davenport in a matter of minutes. But Emma seemed to have been all right with risking that to save his mother. The medicine she brought had lowered his mother's fever within hours, and in the morning, she'd opened her eyes again, asking for water. It was just as incredible as the prostitutes claimed it to be in those rumors that were spreading through the slums of London like wildfire. How had Emma come to such a cure? What was she not telling him? And she said Davenport hadn't hurt her, but was she telling the truth?

He glanced over to his mother, who slept peacefully. Maybe he should just burn the note and never open it. What if it was a sad goodbye note? Something that told him that she cared for him but that they could never be together?

Lady Evergreen opened her eyes for a few seconds but closed them again. John leaned over and kissed her on the forehead.

"Rest, mother. You need to rest more."

He got up and walked over to the fireplace. The flames were dancing wildly, flickering this way and that. He could just let go of the note, feed it to the hungry flames, and never have to worry about Emma again. Try to move on. He loved her with all his heart, and she knew that but had chosen another.

John's fingers loosened their grip around the note, and he was just about to set her free forever when he remembered the look in her eyes whenever he kissed her. Those were the eyes of a woman in love, not a woman who never wanted to see him again. And her coming here last night showed that she still cared for him and his family.

No, something wasn't right here. All the evidence was speaking against Emma, and common sense tried to tell him to let it all go, move on. But as foolish as it sounded, there was a voice stronger than common sense and logic combined, the same voice that had urged him to search for her for months despite her goodbye note. That voice came from the heart and told him loud and clear — *She needs you.*

CHAPTER 14

The carriage stopped in front of a colossal ship that looked like the child of the *Titanic* and a wooden pirate ship. The lower part was made out of steel, but it still had sails and wooden masts. A footman opened the door to the carriage that Emma, Lily, and William were in. William's sister and mother were riding in a different carriage that had already left early in the morning.

Much to Emma's surprise, the harbor was even more chaotic than the busy markets she used to get her bread and cheese from when she was a factory girl. People were moving around like ants, boarding the ship and getting off at the same time. Emma was relieved to see that there was no line for first-class passengers. They were boarded at a different ramp and greeted by the Captain.

Servants who looked like sailors came running and started to unload Emma's trunks from the carriage. At least she didn't have to stand in line with William. The first-class ramp was empty, so she could go straight to her room and retire for the day. Maybe she could even fake seasickness and not have to spend much time with William at all.

William got out of the carriage and offered her his arm. Emma took it without hesitation. She hated his touch, but there was no use in fighting him. It would only anger him, and who knew how that would end. She was afraid of him. Not because of what he could do to her, but because of what he could do to the people she cared about.

William and Emma were already halfway up the ramp to the first-class entrance when she noticed that Lily wasn't behind her any longer. She broke loose from William and turned around. Lily was standing still on the dock, looking left and right, as if she was searching for something. William turned around as well.

"Oh, bloody hell, what is the matter?" he asked in an annoyed tone.

"I...I don't know." She really had no clue.

What had gotten into Lily? Emma was far more devastated about leaving London than Lily was. With this impromptu vacation with William, she worried he might get comfortable pushing his limits and start asking for intimacy.

And…it broke her heart that she would never see John again. So, if someone should have been standing on this dock, it should have been Emma, not Lily.

"Would you excuse me?" Emma said apologetically, leaving William behind and squeezing by two older women who were right behind her on the ramp, trying to board the ship. The ladies mumbled something in disapproval but let her slip by.

"She better hurry up or we shall leave without her," William said loudly enough for her to hear, then continued up the ramp, followed by the two ladies and a few other passengers. Emma had to squeeze by a few more people before she finally reached Lily.

"What's the matter? Skip said he wouldn't see us off to avoid attracting attention."

"That is not it…"

Emma looked up at William, who was waiting on the deck of the ship, keeping a close eye on her.

"Then what is it? William is not a patient man, you know that."

Had Lily lost her mind? By now, she should have known that Emma would have to pay the price for behavior like this. Every time something displeased him, he took away from either Emma's freedom or dignity, and soon there would be absolutely nothing left of either one.

"We just have to wait a little longer," Lily said anxiously.

Emma felt a twinge of sadness as she began to suspect that Lily had decided to stay here. How could she blame her? If Emma had a choice, she would rather be in the poorhouse too than have to spend another day with William, who most likely was not only an abuser but a murderer as well.

"It's fine if you don't want to come along, Lily. I totally understand. I'll send you and Skip money, I promise. It would make me happy to see you free."

Lily's face turned to shock as she huffed, "I would never leave you with that monster!"

Emma grabbed Lily's hands lovingly. "Maybe you should. Just turn around and walk away, Lily. It would mean so much to me to see you free, away from this scumbag."

Emma turned around again to evaluate William's mood, and although he was far away, it was clear that he was now beyond annoyed and becoming deeply angry.

"I have to go," Emma said nervously.

"Please, just wait one more minute!" Lily begged her.

"For what? I can't, Lily. You know how he is. I have to—"

"You are not going anywhere until we clear a few things up first," Emma heard that all too familiar voice say in a tone that would not allow for a maybe.

She couldn't believe it, but there, in between all those people, literally out of nowhere, was John!

Emma felt tears starting to form in her burning eyes. Within seconds, they were running down her face. How did he get here? Was this a dream? All of a sudden, everything that had happened during the last few months came crashing into Emma like the car that had hit her on that devastating night and changed her life forever.

There was no stopping her anymore. To hell with it all. Just a few minutes ago, she had seen her life fading away at the side of an abuser like her father, but then, out of nowhere, the man she loved had come to save her like a knight in shining armor. Without thinking, Emma stormed toward John as if her life depended on it.

"John!" she shouted, throwing herself into his arms so forcefully it could have thrown them both onto the ground if John hadn't been the strong man that he was. He wrapped his arms around her like a shield that would fight the whole world to protect her.

"It is all right. I am here now," John said in that tender voice he reserved for her, melting her heart with each word.

"I'm so sorry. About everything. It's all my fault..." Emma cried into his chest. This could very well be the end of her, but so be it. She was ready to sacrifice herself. Even if this feeling of belonging would only last for a short while, it was worth whatever price she'd have to pay for it.

"That was not a very wise move for such a cunning woman," Emma heard William growl from a few feet away.

His words hit Emma like a punch in the face, and she pulled away from John to turn around and look at him. William's face had hatred written all over it. His jaw was clenched, and his brows furrowed. Emma had never seen him so angry before. William positioned himself, ready to attack, clenching his fists so hard they were shaking. Emma took a frightened step backward. John didn't. Just like on the day they first met, he positioned himself in front of her like he was ready to fight to the bitter end.

"Come on, Davenport! Do it! You cannot even imagine how long I have been waiting for this moment, so please, do me a favor and give me a reason to knock you right out of those fancy boots of yours."

A few people stopped to see what was going on. It wasn't like the whole dock went silent and everybody surrounded them, though—most people went on with their business. Only a handful paused their busy lives to become bystanders. William was trembling with rage now, but he didn't move an inch. Emma couldn't believe it. Why didn't he say or do anything? Call Emma a swindler? Threaten her and Evergreen with ruin?

William just stood there, not making a peep. Was he afraid of John?

"What is the matter, Davenport?" John yelled at him, taking a step toward William, but William did absolutely nothing. John took another step toward him. "What the hell are you waiting for? Come on! Come on, William! Let us finish this, once and for all. You and me!"

But still, William stood silent. He didn't even yell back.

"Just as I thought! Underneath all the glamour and shine is nothing but a coward." John laughed dryly, shaking his head in disgust at William before turning to Emma and Lily. "Let us go. This buffoon is done amusing us for today," John said, loud enough for William and the bystanders to hear.

He offered Emma and Lily each an arm, then gently steered them through the crowd toward his carriage, which waited near a tavern only a few feet away. Lily and Emma constantly looked over their shoulders, as if they expected William to jump out of the crowd and stab them in their backs — literally.

John instructed the driver to take them to his townhouse. The carriage ride was quiet, and John stared at Emma the entire time. Now that her nerves had calmed down a bit, Emma stared back at him. Maybe it was the fact that he had just saved her from a life of misery, but Emma couldn't believe how handsome he was. He was wearing a black day suit, which highlighted his tall, athletic figure. His brown eyes were studying her from head to toe with an intense gaze, causing her to blush. She had no idea what he was thinking, but she knew that he was expecting some answers when they got to a more private place.

The carriage pulled up to the front of a white row house straight out of a historical movie. It must have been a fifth of the size of William's townhouse, but she felt safe and cozy the moment she stepped foot into it.

Lily was smart enough to excuse herself when John led Emma from the entrance hall into a room that must have been the tearoom. It had a fire going in the midst of several chaise lounges and was tastefully decorated with green wallpaper and several paintings. John closed the door behind them and walked over to the fireplace. He waited for a few seconds before turning to face Emma.

"I think you owe me an explanation."

Emma knew he was absolutely right but didn't know where to begin. It didn't help that they were alone in the room, and John looked so incredibly sexy in his slender suit.

"I do. I just don't know where to start."

"The beginning. Please start at the beginning. Who are you?"

Emma wasn't surprised by this question, but it was easier asked than answered. How could she ever tell him the entire truth without sounding like a lunatic? But now that William would ruin both of them, she had to. Especially before John could hear parts of the story elsewhere.

"I would like to start at the end, if that's all right?"

"If it pleases you."

Emma lowered herself to perch on a chaise lounge next to the fireplace. It felt amazing to sit down in a safe place. She had been running for months, never able to rest. She took a deep breath.

"I had to get engaged to William Blackwell because he blackmailed me. He has damaging information on me and threatened to use it to ruin both of us."

John sat down across from her. "Why would he want to ruin me?"

"Because I refused to marry him. I ran from him. That night that I disappeared, I found out that he knew my secret, and I was afraid of him, so I ran. When he found me, I was at a point in life with little left to lose. The threat of ruin did not scare me at all, so he had to change his strategy. He knew how much I cared for you—"

"Are you saying you agreed to marry that monster in order to save me from ruin?" John interrupted her. He looked shocked.

"I had already hurt you and your family enough. I knew I could never marry you, but at least I could let you and your family live in dignity and peace."

"Peace? I have not slept since the night you disappeared, leaving nothing behind but a thank-you note, Emma! I blamed myself for everything. My whole life, I have never cared for nor touched a woman. You were the first I ever wanted to be with, so I took things too far too soon. Then you left in the middle of the night, and after what had happened between us, I thought it was all my fault. I hated myself. I combed through London one backstreet at a time, always one step behind

Davenport, not knowing if you were in good health or if I was the reason you were running. Does that sound peaceful to you?"

Emma shook her head.

"And now I find out that all of that was to save my reputation? To hell with my reputation — I love you!" John was angry.

Understandable, considering what Emma had done to him.

She started to wonder if she had made the right decision when she tried to protect him. She had made decisions for him, hidden who she really was, treated him like a little child who needed protection when, in reality, she was the one who needed protection. As her mother always said, selflessness is good as long as it doesn't hurt others.

"I'm so sorry, John. I should have come to you, talked to you. It was just that..." Emma stopped. It was so hard to tell him the truth. What if he hated her? She wasn't sure if she could survive that.

"What, Emma? Just tell me. If you cared for me, why was it so impossible to consider marriage to me? I sure as hell would have made a better husband than Davenport. I mean, we made love, for God's sake!"

This was it. Now or never, Emma.

"I faked the robbery to get the duke to fall in love with me and marry me." She was just as shocked hearing those words come out of her mouth as John was. It made her sound awful. Like the worst person on this planet.

John just looked at her without saying a word.

"But then I met you, and it didn't seem right to marry him. So, I rejected his proposal. I really loved you, wanted to be with you. You do believe me about that, John, don't you?" Emma stood up and took a step toward him, as if she wanted to see if he would still be able to tolerate her.

John didn't move, not toward her but also not away from her.

"Why would you do such a thing? For money? Then why turn my proposal down as well? Sure, I am not as rich as the duke is, but I am not struggling either." John threw both of his arms up, pointing out the fine room they were sitting in as proof of his financial stability. "None of this makes sense, Emma. What is it you are not telling me? You are not a fortune hunter. I know that. So why would you fake a robbery to get to money and privilege?"

Emma threw her face into her hands. "Because I'm not who you think I am. I'm not from the America you know. I'm from a different America. A different time... I'm from the future!" Emma shouted in despair, looking back up to see how John would process this confession.

He stood up silently. Panic hit Emma like a hurricane making landfall. Was he leaving? Calling the police to lock her up? Maybe into an insane asylum? But John did neither. He calmly walked over to the fireplace to look into its flames for a few seconds before he turned around again.

"From the future..." he repeated, shaking his head.

Emma hastened over to him. "I know this sounds crazy, but you have to believe me."

"Emma... I..." John started, staring at her with brows raised, as though he was looking for words.

Emma interrupted him. "Just think about it. All those games I taught you and your family that you have never heard of. Think of all those stories every night about airplanes and dinosaurs. Those aren't stories from America in 1881. Those are real things from the future. Well, not the dinosaurs, but everything else I told you about."

"Yes, but—"

"And the penicillin. The medicine I gave your mother and used to cure the women in the slums of London. How would I know about such a miracle cure? It won't be discovered until 1928," Emma said in a tone that sounded incredibly desperate.

As crazy as she knew she sounded, John appeared to actually be thinking about what Emma was telling him, as if he was debating with himself whether she was telling the truth or not. He could have burst out in laughter, called her insane, told her to leave. All understandable and natural reactions, considering all she had said. But not John.

Emma grabbed her purse from the chaise longue and pulled her cell phone out. Looking at the cell with all the curiosity in the world, John came closer as she turned it on. The familiar welcome sound rang, and the screen lit up, displaying a picture of Emma and her dog.

Emma handed it to John. "This is called a cell phone. Where I am from, everybody has one."

John turned and twisted her cell, touching the screen with an expression that could only be described as pure marvel. Emma swiped over the display to unlock it. She went into her picture gallery and showed him how to swipe through the pictures. This was something she and Lily had only done when they were desperate for something to keep them going, as she was always worried about her battery life.

"This is my world, John. See for yourself."

John fell backward onto the chaise lounge, staring at the phone in disbelief. He flipped through the gallery, pulling up pictures of Emma with friends, at the park, and many other places. He stopped at a photo that showed Emma in a car with her mother. "Is this your mother?"

"Yes." Emma felt that all too familiar knot in her throat. Her poor mother must think her dead. Just like everybody else. "She is still in the future. I came here alone."

"How...what... What happened?"

Did that mean he believed her? Emma sat down next to him. "I don't know. I walked home from a party and was hit by a car. All I remember is waking up here, in London in 1881. Lily found me when that Flinch guy tried to rob me."

"A car?"

"That thing here," she pointed at the picture. "It's like a carriage without a horse, powered by an engine like a train. It hit me and made me come here. How, I don't know."

"So, you tried to get Davenport to marry you to be able to find a way back home?"

"Yes. Where I'm from, women are allowed to study and make money on their own. Enough to support themselves."

"Something that is a rate privilege to women of society in my time. So that is why you wanted to become the Duchess of Davenport."

"It wasn't an honorable plan, but I was desperate. I just wanted to go back home. Then you came along, and I...I fell in love with you. That night in your room, I wanted to tell you the truth, to let you choose for yourself if you still wanted to be with me. But then you talked about Elise and how she was not the woman you thought she was."

John smiled sadly. "And that reminded you of yourself, thinking I would not want anything to do with you anymore."

"Pretty much."

John put her cell next to him on the chaise lounge and turned to Emma.

"Emma, there is a big difference between a woman cheating on her fiancé and then deliberately trying to destroy his family out of spite, and a woman who was torn away from her home and loved ones, trying desperately to go back home under circumstances that force her to lie." John moved closer to her, taking her hand into his.

Emma's heart began to thud as she finally let herself feel true hope.

"Emma, I do not even know what to say. This must have been so hard for you. All of it. So far from your family, living in poverty, Davenport … Me… It breaks my heart to think about all the pain you must have been through."

His words touched her, and the warmth of his hand around hers made her feel beyond grateful. Tears started to roll down her face, though she tried to be strong. "I've survived worse. Plus, you were one of the few people who kept me going."

John moved closer to Emma and took her into his arms. It felt so good to finally be held as the woman she was, by the man she loved. Not an heiress from America looking for an estate but Emma Washington, a PhD student from the twenty-first century.

John leaned back a bit to be able to look into her eyes. "Emma, I still love you. I always have and always will."

She felt those butterflies in her stomach again. That incredible feeling she only felt with John and thought she would never feel again. She could feel his breath on her. Her heart was beating faster and faster.

"I love you too, John. With all my heart." She leaned in and kissed him, her burning lips gently touching the warmth of his. He kissed her back, softly at first, then with a passion that parted her trembling lips, sending tremors through both of them.

"Will you marry me, then?" he whispered into her ear before pressing his mouth onto her red, swollen lips again.

"I will," she moaned back at him, still attached to his lips. Emma felt the wet lust between her legs again, the very same she felt every time their bodies touched. Her breathing grew heavier as she pulled him against her, wrapping her arms around the man she loved.

Suddenly, somebody knocked at the door. John barely pulled away from Emma.

"Go away," he shouted, smiling at Emma, who melted at the thought of being undisturbed with him.

"Emma, it is me." Lily's voice came through the door.

Emma sat up straight and pushed John away with a grin. He gave her a quick last kiss before the door opened.

Lily looked at them, crossing her arms. "It would be nice if someone could find the time to tell me if Davenport is planning to kill me. I'm scared to death, sitting all by myself in the kitchen."

God, poor Lily. She had totally forgotten about her. Emma didn't know how to answer this question and turned to her savior to see if John had a prediction.

"Davenport will do no such thing. He will do nothing, to be precise."

"Nothing?" both Emma and Lily asked at the same time.

John grinned. "Nothing."

"But what about telling everybody who I am and ruining your family?"

"Ha! If Davenport had that kind of power, he would have ruined me every time I hurt his big ego in a shooting competition."

John's word confused Emma, which she expressed clearly on her face.

"He knows I have letters from him. Letters in which he tells me that I can have Elise back if I wish. Letters in which he is begging me never to tell anybody about him and Elise, to save him from a scandal."

Emma turned white like a ghost. "So, his whole threat to destroy you was…"

"Nothing but a trick. Hot air. It is the only thing he is good at. Lies and tricks."

Emma felt so stupid. She had almost married a man who was like her father because he had used the same skillset as her father. Lying, cheating, and tricks.

Lily let out a huge cry of relief. "Oh, thank God!" she said, face up to the sky as if she were thanking God in person.

"Besides, that little meater is terrified of me."

"Meater?"

"Coward. There is not a single match that has ever taken place between the two of us where I did not win. Fencing, boxing, shooting. He would not dare to challenge me."

Emma's voice returned at last, and her shock turned to anger. "That piece of shit! I will kill him myself!"

John laughed. "I like it when you get mad, Lady Evergreen. Shows your passion."

Emma blushed.

"Lady Evergreen?" Lily asked, with the biggest smile Emma had ever seen on her face.

John grabbed Emma's hand and kissed it. "Yes, Lady Evergreen," he repeated.

"Oh, Emma, I am so delighted!" Lily came running and threw herself into Emma's arms.

Emma glanced over to John, who looked deeply happy. Right then and there, holding her best friend close to her heart, looking at the man she loved more than herself, Emma felt a sense of happiness and belonging unlike any she had ever felt before. There was only one person missing right now who would make her family complete.

"Let's go get our chuckaboo, Skip," Emma said.

Lily jumped up, still grinning. "Chuckaboo indeed. Yes, let us go get him!"

John looked at them in confusion. "The carriage driver?" he asked, drawing his brows together.

"Yes, the carriage driver," Emma said, laughing out loud.

EPILOGUE

The wind was blowing harshly, pulling out little strands of Emma's hair from her neatly tied bun. She was standing on the Brooklyn bridge, staring at the Statue of Liberty with a feeling of deep nostalgia.

"I didn't think I would ever see you again," she whispered into the wind to the statue that she had seen so many times before, but never with so much appreciation. Emma slowly caressed her belly in a gesture of love for the child she was carrying inside her. For the past two years, Emma had followed every lead she could to find a way home, but all she had stumbled upon was a statement by a newspaper boy that left her with more questions than answers. According to the boy, the night Emma was hit by a car, a lady was seen bending over, picking something up in the middle of the road, before getting hit by a carriage. The boy swore by all that was holy that she had just disappeared right then and there. All of this had happened on the same street where Emma was found.

That was all she was ever able to find out about the mysterious accident that had changed her life forever. To be fair, Emma had stopped looking for a way home long before she openly gave up her research. Her home wasn't in the twenty-first century any longer. It was here at the side of the man she loved. The man who had reassured her that he would rather be with her for a limited time than not at all. And now, after all these years, she'd finally made it back home.

"It's cold, let's go home," John said, hugging her from behind and placing a tender kiss on her cheek. Emma nestled her head against his shoulder for a moment, closing her eyes in disbelief at how much love and happiness the human heart was capable of. It had been John's idea to move to America, for the woman he loved so dearly, but also to thank the country that had given him the love of his life.

"Yes, let's go home."

Philadelphia, present day.

Somebody was knocking at the door to Lauren Washington's apartment. Emma had been missing for about a week. Like every mother of a missing child, Lauren was beside herself, worried to the point of insanity. She bolted to the door, praying it was the police with information about Emma.

She opened the door, but it wasn't the police. Lauren's heart almost stopped. In front of her stood a young woman who looked so much like her Emma, it could have been her twin sister. There were a few differences in the facial features and in height, but the colors of her hair and eyes were exactly those of her Emma.

"Who...are you?" Lauren stammered in disbelief.

"Are you Lauren Washington? Emma's mother?" the woman asked in a kind voice.

"Y-yes."

"My name is Jasmin. Jasmin Evergreen."

"Jasmin Evergreen? D-do I know you?"

"It is complicated," the woman said with a smile. "May I come in?"

Still unable to understand what was going on, Lauren opened the door wide enough to let Jasmin in.

Jasmin took a quick peek around the room. It was a small studio with old furniture, all Lauren could afford after finally leaving Emma's father. She often felt ashamed for not leaving him sooner, but she was also proud of herself for leaving at all.

"Please, sit down," Lauren said, but Jasmin walked over to her and handed her a small antique box.

"You should read the letter first. It is in the box. My number is written on a card in there as well. Call me when you are done reading the letter. It's all explained in there."

With that, Jasmin walked straight to the apartment's door and left.

Lauren was speechless. What was going on here? Who was this woman? And why did she look like her Emma? She opened the box to discover a key and a letter that looked like it was very old. She held the letter close to her face.

"'To Mother,'" Lauren read out loud before opening it. She almost dropped it the moment she recognized the script. This was Emma's handwriting, no doubt! But how was this possible? And who was this Jasmin?

Lauren read the first sentences of the letter out loud to make sure none of this was a dream...

"'Dear Mother, you might be worried about me, but please don't be. I am safe and happier than I have ever been. If everything goes well, one of my descendants will hand you the very box you are holding in your hand. Please sit down, as you are about to read the craziest romance story of your life, and also find out that this key leads to a whole bunch of money set aside for you...'"

OUT NOW!

The second and third book in the Time Travel Series are out on Amazon:

https://www.amazon.com/dp/B084MNW7DB
(Both FREE with Kindle Unlimited!)

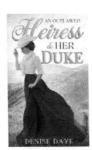

https://www.amazon.com/dp/B0867QCBXF

Feel like something more contemporary?

THANK YOU!

First of all, thank you for purchasing Trapped in Time. I know you could have picked any number of books to read, but you picked this book, and for that, I am extremely grateful. As a small-time author and a full-time mom, my readers mean a lot to me!

If you enjoyed this book, it would be really nice if you could leave a review for this book on Amazon. You can review the book here:

https://www.amazon.com/dp/B083N237V9

Your feedback and support will help me to continue writing romance novels.

Also, don't forget to sign up for my newsletter to get alerts of FREE novels. You can find the newsletter and more info about my books here:

www.timelesspapers.com

Thank you!

ABOUT THE AUTHOR

Denise graduated with a master's in Social Work from an ivy league school and has spent many years of her life working with families and individuals in need of assistance. She has always had a passion for writing, but it wasn't until her own baby boy was born that Denise turned her passion into her profession. Whenever Denise is not typing away on one of her books, you can find her caring for her son (a.k.a. one of the toughest jobs in the world), binging Netflix with her beloved husband, or chasing after her puppy (who should technically be an adult dog by now).

Made in the USA
Middletown, DE
04 November 2021